DEADLY CLIENT

JENNA ST. JAMES

Deadly Client

Jenna St. James

Copyright © 2021 by Jenna St. James.

Published by Jenna St. James

All Rights Reserved. No part of this publication may be reproduced without the written permission of the author.

This is a work of fiction. Names and characters are either the product of the author's imagination or are used fictitiously, and any resemblance to actual persons, living or dead, business establishments, events, or locales is entirely coincidental.

❀ Created with Vellum

Chapter One

༺❀༻

"*Is this our last stop for the day?*" Needles asked as he sat perched on the roof of my ancient beat-up Bronco, his wings shimmering baby blue. "*I could use a nap.*"

I waved my hand in the air and used my magic to close the tailgate. "Then stay here and take a nap."

"*You know I can't do that, Princess,*" Needles said. "*I am your bodyguard, and it's my duty to protect you. Black Forest King insists.*"

I rolled my eyes at his ridiculous statement. I'd recently retired from a government agency where taking down bad-guy supernaturals was my job. I was also one of the highest ranking agents they'd had…which meant I was more than capable of handling myself. But ever since I retired and came back home to Enchanted Island to serve as the game warden, my dad—Black Forest King—insisted Needles watch over me twenty-four seven.

"Then I guess you better perk up, Porcupine, because I got work to do. It's not even lunchtime yet."

Needles wasn't your typical bodyguard. He was a flying and

talking porcupine who stood just five inches tall and had oversized wings that changed colors to suit his mood. I was one of only two supernaturals—besides my father—who could hear Needles speak. The other person was Zoie Stone...the daughter of my current boyfriend and sheriff of Enchanted Island.

"I'm just saying," Needles whined, *"this is the fourth day doing the same thing over and over again. I'm quite bored, Princess."*

I was anything but bored. For the first time *ever,* my dad had granted access to enter the north side of the island for the specific purpose of gathering data on all the flora, fauna, and natural land formations. By my calculation, I had nearly one hundred thousand acres of uninhibited forest to trek through. It would take months, not days.

My dad, Black Forest King, was a genius loci. That meant he was literally the heart and soul of Black Forest...an impenetrable location made up of a hundred acres just a mile from my house. One of the conditions he set—before allowing supernaturals looking to flee the mainland in fear for their lives and to live on the island nearly four hundred years ago—was that no one would enter the north side of the island. A deal was struck between Dad and a handful of witches all those years ago. And for the most part, the citizens of Enchanted Island had adhered to that agreement made by their ancestors—mainly because just the mention of Black Forest King struck fear in the hearts of many supernatural island citizens.

Most genius loci had that ability.

"Well, get your bored butt off my roof," I said, "and let's go."

I slung my backpack over my shoulder, slipped on a pair of latex gloves for sample collecting, and headed toward the forested area where I wanted to take data. From what Dad had told me, this section contained a large clearing that housed both a natural waterfall and a geyser. Even though the north side of the island wasn't included as part of Black Forest, my dad still had a strong connection to it and the island as a whole.

We'd hiked about a mile when I finally came to a large clearing. Ducking down beneath a branch, I stood and gasped. The view was absolutely spectacular. A cascading waterfall, probably seven stories high, flowed from a rocky ledge overhead. The roar of the gigantic waterfall was deafening, and the beauty of the myriad flowers that surrounded the base of the river took my breath away.

Needles sprang from my shoulder, zipped to the middle of the river close to the waterfall, did a somersault, then dipped down low until his wing touched the water. With a whoop, he rocketed down the middle of the churning river, water spraying in all directions as he sailed by.

I laughed and shook my head at his childlike antics. I wasn't exactly sure how old Needles was, but he'd been sent by my father to watch over me in the crib, and every once in a while, Needles would talk of things I knew to be long ago. I guessed him to be maybe two hundred years old. But I wasn't sure. I'm not even sure if Needles knew how old he was.

"Silly porcupine," I called out. "You aren't getting in my Bronco soaking wet."

Needles flew over to where I knelt near the edge of the water, unloading my sample bottles and notebook, and shook his body over me, covering me in water.

"You little—"

I reached up and tried to snatch him out of the air, but he was too fast. Laughing, he zipped over to a boulder about ten yards away and proceeded to sun himself.

"I'll get you back," I said. "When you least expect it."

"Yeah, yeah."

His eyes were closed, so I didn't think he took my threat seriously. I tested the pH level of the river, and had just started collecting petals of unknown flowers, when I felt movement under my feet.

"What's that?" I hollered over at the sunbathing Needles.

Needles' eyes flew open, and he zipped over to me. *"Stand back, Princess. The geyser is about to blow."*

My head whipped from side to side. "What geyser? I don't see a geyser."

Before Needles could answer, a cloud of steam shot out from the ground about twenty feet from where I stood. A few seconds later, water shot in the air.

"That's hot," I said, taking a step back.

"Of course it's hot," Needles said. *"It's coming from the ground."*

I rolled my eyes. "I know the water is warmed by geothermal heat, Needles. I just didn't realize how hot it would be. It's one thing to read about…it's another to experience."

I watched in amazement as the water continued to shoot out of the ground. I took a step forward, eager to get a little closer. I'd taken a few more steps before I stumbled backward.

"That smell!" I slapped a gloved hand over my mouth and nose.

"Rotten eggs," Needles laughed, his wings shimmering purple. *"The island's way of telling you to back off."*

As quickly as it erupted, it died down just as fast.

"That was amazing," I said. "I can't believe this area is so close to the edge of the north side of the island where citizens aren't supposed to cross. If one person ever stumbled upon this, we'd never keep anyone out."

"The fear of the unknown was easier to wield hundreds of years ago," Needles said. *"Supernaturals today aren't as fearful.*

They don't know what it's like to flee somewhere to escape persecution. To respect the agreement made by their ancestors."

My cell phone rang. I yanked off my glove and fished it out of my pocket.

"Hey, Alex." I turned my back on Needles so I could have some privacy. "What's up?"

"Just thought I'd call and see how you're coming along," Alex said.

More than anything, I wanted to tell him about what I'd just witnessed. But I knew I couldn't. If word ever got out there was a waterfall and geyser that bordered the north side of the island, it would be my fault.

"Good," I said. "I've gathered samples of flowers I don't recognize. I'll show them to Dad and ask him about them."

"None of them poisonous, I hope?" Alex mused.

We'd had our fair share of run-ins with poisonous plants on the island and knew first-hand how dangerous they could be. "Not that I know of."

"That's not very reassuring," Alex muttered.

"Don't worry. I know how dangerous the north side of the island can be. I'm being cautious."

"I know you are," Alex said. "Doesn't stop me from worrying about you."

I smiled. "I like hearing that. So, did you call for a specific reason? Or just to hear my voice?"

He chuckled. "A little of both. Do you know Nate Howler or his family? Werewolves?"

"Not off the top of my head."

"I just received a call from Nate's roommate, Jordan Owlman. He claims Nate has gone missing. But here's the kicker—even though both guys live on the island, they're staying at some place called The Spellmoore."

"The Spellmoore?" I frowned and thought about where I was located on the map. "I'll have to double-check, but I think I'm only like a mile or two from there right now."

"I have little in terms of details," Alex said. "The roommate just said Nate hadn't shown for a morning meeting, and no one can find him. He thought he should call the police."

"I can meet you at The Spellmoore in about thirty," I said.

"What about your samples?" Alex asked.

I snorted. "Witch, remember? I can keep them in my backpack at the exact temperature they need to be for as long as I need to."

"Gargoyle, remember? I forget that kind of stuff is possible."

I laughed. "I adore you. I'll see you soon."

Chapter Two

I disconnected and slipped the phone back in the pants pocket of my uniform.

"What's going on?" Needles asked. *"I never thought I'd say this, but do we finally have a case?"*

"Maybe. Missing person." I jogged over to where I'd left my samples, whispered a temperature-control spell over each small jar, and shoved them in my backpack.

"We aren't too far from where he's staying," I said. "We can hike out of here, grab my Bronco, and be at The Spellmoore in about half an hour."

An eastern tiger swallowtail butterfly floated down and hovered near my face. "Hello, beautiful girl."

"Hello, Princess."

I blinked in surprise. Usually, animals outside Black Forest didn't speak to me verbally. I just picked up on their emotions. A hereditary gift from Dad.

"Is everything all right?" I asked, lifting my hand up so she could perch on my fingertips.

"No, Princess. I've been sent to tell you something is wrong in the river."

Needles zipped over to us. *"What's wrong?"*

The butterfly flapped her wings, and I could feel her anxiety now. *"I'm not sure. Something isn't where it's supposed to be."*

"What do you mean?" I asked.

The butterfly quivered on my fingertips. *"I don't know exactly, Princess."*

Because her anxiety was almost crippling, I whispered a soothing spell and lightly brushed my other hand over her wings. "You are safe here, little butterfly. Do not fear."

Needles zipped to the top of the waterfall, then returned a minute later. *"There's unrest on top. No animal can tell me exactly what the problem is, but when they realized you were in the forest, they banded together to get a message to you."*

I looked over my shoulder in the direction I'd parked the Bronco, about a mile back. Then looked up about seven stories to the top of the waterfall and sighed. "I guess I levitate to the top and come back later for the Bronco?"

"Agreed," Needles said, his wings shimmering greenish-blue. *"We need to hurry."*

The butterfly thanked me and flew from my fingertips.

Sliding on the backpack, I jogged over to the base of the cliff where the water cascaded down, closed my eyes, whispered the levitation spell, and slowly started to rise. Usually, I only needed to lift something or myself a story or two in the air, so this was a little scary.

I breathed a sigh of relief when the crest line—a rocky embankment—came into view. Even though the waterfall was a good ten feet away from me, I knew the edge would be slippery. When I was eye level with the rocks, I reached out and lifted myself over the ledge and onto the embankment.

Standing, I sidestepped out of the wet rocks and onto the grassy ridge. A part of me wanted to look over and see how far down it was to the bottom, but the other part of me was afraid I'd get dizzy and fall. Common sense won out, and I hiked over to where Needles and the butterfly hovered in the air, waiting for me.

"I can't be sure how far up ahead it is," Needles said, *"but it's definitely up ahead in the stream."*

I elected to jog the forest floor along the edge of the river surrounded by the trees, while Needles and the butterfly flew above the rocky, churning water. A rabbit and squirrel joined in on the hunt and ran alongside me.

The farther we went, the calmer the river became. There was a bend to the right about ten yards ahead, but my gaze was on the fallen log in the river. Something large was trapped in the branches.

"I see it," I called out to Needles.

He and the butterfly flew my way. I looked up the embankment south of the river and frowned at the wall of rocks in the distance.

"What's with the rocks?" I asked. "They don't look natural."

"We're on the edge of the north forest," Needles said. *"This river marks where citizens can't roam. That's why the embankment on the north is packed with pine trees. Nothing is getting through there that shouldn't. Not without a fight, anyway. I'd say those rocks to the south are a barrier put up by a supernatural."*

"I'm going to wade out, but I'm not going to haul it in," I said. "I think I know what it is."

I slowly made the climb over the river's slippery rocks, holding on to the log to make sure I didn't fall. The water was colder than I expected, and the churning rapids nearly tipped me over. When I came to the lump stuck in the tree branches, I bent down to look—then quickly stood.

Yanking my cell phone out of my pocket, I dialed Alex's number. "Hey, it's me. I think I found Nate Howler."

Chapter Three

"How did you find him?" Alex asked. "Are we on the north side of the island?"

"Sort of," I said. "Technically, the river marks the start of the border, where supernaturals aren't to roam. That's why there's a steep embankment with a fortress of trees to the north of the river."

"It's weird," Grant said, frowning and scratching his head as he watched the rushing water. "Usually water doesn't flow this way."

"I caught that too," Alex said. "Doesn't make sense."

"Welcome to Enchanted Island, boys," Needles said from my shoulder.

I laughed. "It's Enchanted Island. It's not always supposed to make sense. But, yeah, this isn't normal. Dad cut this huge swath here to designate the border. It pretty much snakes west to east."

"Very weird," Grant muttered.

"I have the body in the ambulance," Doc said.

The three of us turned at Doc Drago's statement. Doc was the medical examiner for Enchanted Island, and a dragon shifter. He came in double-handy today.

"I'm sorry you had to do that," Alex said. "But I didn't see any other way to get the body over those massive boulders and to the ambulance."

"I understand," Doc said. "And you made the right call."

When it became apparent the werewolf and vampire paramedics couldn't safely carry out the body on a stretcher because they'd had to climb over the massive man-made rock barrier, Doc had volunteered to shift to his dragon form and carry out the stretcher.

"I just can't believe it's Nate Howler," Doc said. "His parents will be devastated."

Once the body had been removed from the branches, it had been searched. Nate's wallet was on him. But the icing on the cake came when Alex pulled out an electronic device no bigger than a phone, pulled a hair from the body, and scanned it. Ten minutes later, a positive ID came back. It was Nate Howler. Alex could have also scanned fingerprints on the device, but Nate's fingertips had been too waterlogged to get an accurate read.

The new scanning device had been rolled out by the forensic IT guy, Gordon Hoots, last week. He claimed it was eighty percent technology and twenty percent magic. However he'd created it...it was genius. Now Alex and Grant could ID someone and get an instant identification—provided said information was in the supernatural database.

"I'm going to go give Mr. and Mrs. Howler the news," Grant said. "I know the Howlers well. They were one of the first werewolf families to welcome me into the pack when I showed signs of shifting."

"Good," Doc said. "They will appreciate that. I have tentative

TOD around eleven last night to four this morning. I'll know more when the autopsy is complete."

"I think we know cause of death," I said. "The knife sticking out of his chest being a good guess."

Doc gave me a small smile. "Yes, I'm thinking that might be cause of death. But again, until I perform the autopsy, I won't know for sure. Could be someone poisoned him first or did something else to incapacitate him. Every little bit helps."

"Shayla," Alex said, "do me a favor and text those photos you took of the knife to my phone. That way, we both have them. I want to see if the knife came from The Spellmoore."

"On it."

I quickly did as he requested.

"If you don't need me anymore," Grant said. "I think I'll go speak with the Howlers."

Alex nodded. "I appreciate it. Let me know what they say. I'm going to talk with the owner of the property, see what she can tell me, speak with the roommate, get his statement. See if they know who would want to hurt Mr. Howler. Hopefully, I'll have a list of persons of interest needing background information you can run shortly."

"Sounds good," Grant said.

"I'll walk back with you, Grant," Doc said. "But first, I feel I need to warn you, Sheriff. You haven't been on the island long, so you probably don't know. I heard Jordan Owlman called the station to report Nate missing. Jordan is Gordon Hoot's nephew on his sister's side."

"Our computer forensics specialist?" Alex asked. "The guy who just made the ID thing?"

"The one and only," Doc said.

I gave a low whistle. "This just got sticky."

"Thanks for the heads up," Alex said.

After they both left, Alex turned to me and lifted an eyebrow. "I suppose you'll want to join in on the investigation?"

"I think *technically* this might be *my* investigation. After all, I found Nate in a body of water *and* said body of water is an island landmark." I shrugged. "I could make an argument this is my case, but I'm willing to give the nod to you."

"Good one, Princess," Needles said, doing a little twirl in the air, his wings shimmering greenish-yellow. *"Show him who's boss."*

Alex sent Needles a glare. "I probably don't want to know what he said, do I?"

"Nope," I said.

"In light of your informative argument," Alex said, "I guess I should thank you for offering me the lead on this investigation."

"I'm giving like that," I deadpanned.

Alex laughed. "C'mon. Let's go see what the owner of this magnificent hotel has to say."

I knew of The Spellmoore, of course. Having been raised on the island, there wasn't much of anyplace I didn't know about. But I'd never been to The Spellmoore. It was a resort for vacationing supernaturals who lived on the mainland to stay…not actual citizens of Enchanted Island.

Alex and I scrambled up the small embankment, then scaled the large, three-foot boulders that wanted to block our every move.

When we finally reached the petite, middle-aged woman pacing back and forth on a narrow cement path, I was sweating and breathing hard. But my irritation quickly evaporated when the woman turned her agony-filled eyes on us.

"My name is Melody Spellmoore. I'm the owner of the hotel. Can you please tell me what's going on?"

Chapter Four

"Ms. Spellmoore," Alex said, "I'm Sheriff Stone, and this is my partner, Agent Loci. We'd like to ask you a couple questions."

"Of course," she said. "I just don't understand what's going on. No one is telling me anything. My staff informed me the cops were driving around on the property, and when I stepped outside, I saw an ambulance race by me and head to the back portion of my property." She started to wring her hands. "Guests are demanding to know what's going on, but I don't know what to say."

Alex held up his hand. "I'm sorry for any damage we may have done to your grass back here."

Melody waved her hand dismissively in the air. "I don't care about my grass. I just want to know what's going on."

"Deputy Sparks was supposed to explain everything to you," Alex said. "You two must have missed each other."

"We must have," Melody said. "Perhaps he's up at the hotel."

I glanced around. Now that I wasn't so focused on not falling over rocks, I took in my surrounding. Acres of flat, green grass had been carved out from the encroaching forest, making it easy for guests to walk and explore. Behind me were the twenty yards of giant rocks we'd just climbed over. Trees lined the walkway, giving shade. Wooden structures popped up sporadically over the landscape, but I couldn't tell what they were.

"How many acres do you have here?" I asked.

"Thirty," Melody said. "My great-great-grandfather built the place years ago. We've added on over the years, but he's the one who first had the idea for The Spellmoore."

"And the rocks?" I asked.

Melody nodded. "That was also my great-great-grandpa's idea. He knew how close we were to the border, so to encourage no trespassing, he had the rocks brought in. He knew the rule about no one on the north side of the island, as did my father, and now myself. That's why we've kept them there all this time."

Alex took out a mini notebook from his pocket. "Earlier today, the sheriff's station received a call about a missing person. I notified Agent Loci—Enchanted Island's game warden—who was taking data around these parts. She agreed to meet me here."

When Alex nodded to me, I picked up where he left off. "As I ran down the river and neared the bend, I saw something—a body—tangled in the branches of a fallen tree trunk."

Melody's mouth dropped. "Someone fell in? But that's impossible. How? Who?"

"That's the strange part," Alex said. "It's a local man who lives on the island."

Melody frowned. "He's a citizen of Enchanted Island? Not a guest?"

"You tell us," I said. "Do you know Nate Howler?"

Melody gasped and covered her mouth. "Yes, I know Nate. He fell in? He's *dead*?" She closed her eyes and shook her head.

"You're right. He lives on the island, but he's staying here. He and his business partner, Jordan, are both staying here. They have this big presentation this week."

"What kind of presentation?" Alex asked, looking up from his notebook where he'd been scribbling notes.

"I'm sure I won't explain it correctly, but from what I understand, Nate and Jordan came up with an app you can put on your phone. They're now trying to sell it to three different supernatural companies. Those companies sent someone to negotiate terms or whatever to buy this app, and those three people are also staying at The Spellmoore. It's a pretty big deal." A tear fell down her cheek. "How could this have happened?"

"When was the last time you saw Nate?" Alex asked.

Melody frowned and looked up, as though she were thinking. "I'd say last night. Yes, Wednesday night. I strolled through the restaurant around eight-thirty and saw him with his girlfriend. They were having dinner together."

Alex looked up from his notepad. "Do you know the girlfriend or know her name?"

Melody shook her head. "Not really. I think her name is Anya, but I'm not sure."

"Is she staying at The Spellmoore too?"

"No. She's just dropping by at night. Well, to be honest, I'm afraid I was going to have to say something to her the next time I saw her."

"About what?" I asked.

Melody hesitated. "I'd normally never discuss something so openly, but I guess you should know. Nate's girlfriend is causing trouble for one of the women who flew in and is part of the negotiations for the boys' app." She held up her hands. "You better ask those involved what's going on. I only know what I'm getting second hand from my employees and from the girl who is being harassed. She can better explain."

Alex nodded. "Okay. What is the woman's name who is being harassed?"

"Gracie Pixman."

"Pixman?" I frowned. "Like the Pixmans who used to live on the island?"

"Probably," Melody said. "Gracie told me she grew up on the island."

I frowned. "Fairy, right?"

"I believe so," Melody said. "But her parents moved to the mainland when Gracie was in high school."

I took my cell out and showed her a picture of the knife, doing my best to enlarge the photo so she didn't have to see the body. "Do you recognize this knife?"

Tears filled Melody's eyes, and she slowly shook her head back and forth. "I don't understand what's going on. I'm almost positive that's one of our kitchen knives. One of our kitchen staff reported it missing this morning. I get them special ordered from George Werely. He's a bladesmith here on the island. Sort of famous, actually." She pointed to a spot on the knife. "See the symbol right there? That's his special mark for The Spellmoore. Makes it unique."

Alex and I both knew who George Werely was. We'd had a run-in with him awhile back on our first case together. George was half werewolf-half giant. And Melody was correct—George and his blades were famous in the supernatural world.

I turned and looked across the expanse of the boulders on the ground. I couldn't see the drop-off where the river ran because of the height of the rocks, but I could definitely see the tall pines on the other side of the river. Those that blocked the entrance to the north side of the island.

"So your guests can only get this close to the river?" I asked. "Where we are standing now on the cement path? There's no other way—outside of climbing over those huge rocks—to get to the edge of the river?"

Melody's eyes went wide. "I just realized what might have happened. See, I have these magic carpets that—"

Alex held up his hand. "You have magic carpets?"

"I'd forgotten about the magic carpets," I murmured. "It's been years since I thought of those. GiGi told me about enchanting them when I was a little girl."

Melody smiled. "It was something my grandparents did. And, yes, I believe GiGi had a part in it."

I nodded. "GiGi was a young witch at the time. I don't remember now if it was her coven or just a few of the witches that helped your grandparents with the spell, but she told me stories of flying around on carpets."

"That's right. My grandparents, along with five or six other witches, enchanted magic carpets *years* ago as a way for guests to tour the resort without having to walk everywhere." She shrugged. "Magic carpets added to the magical element of The Spellmoore. I can show you, if you like?"

"This I want to see," Alex said.

"I'm going to go speak to the trees and animals," Needles said. *"See what they can tell me."*

Up until that point, Needles had been silently listening to Melody answer our questions. I nodded, and Needles took off toward a cluster of trees and shrubs on the other side of the walkway.

"They are kept in these structures," Melody said, leading us to one of the wooden buildings I'd noticed earlier.

The sidewalk curved, giving us the choice to continue straight or to veer off to the shed. We veered off and stopped in front of the short building. There were four open bays, and each bay held two magic carpets. A narrow door was off to the side.

A young man stepped forward. "The two that were out are now back."

"Thank you, Harper," Melody said. "You may return to your original duty."

He nodded and hurried away.

"When I saw the police down here," Melody said, "I radioed to the hotel and had them send someone down to stand guard. There were two carpets out, but Harper tracked them down and had them returned."

"Were they near where we were?" Alex asked.

Melody shook her head. "No, they were farther down. Between the river and the golf range. Nowhere near where you found the body."

We stepped farther inside, and I couldn't believe what I was seeing.

"Amazing," I whispered, bending down to run my hand over one of the multi-colored Persian rugs.

"Thank you," Melody said. "All you have to do is sit down on the rug and it automatically lifts you in the air. To make it move, you just tell it where to go."

"Who can take them out?" Alex asked.

"Anyone. They are always available to guests." She shrugged. "We've never had an incident with them, so I've never thought to close them away or lock them up at night. No one usually messes with them after dark anyway."

I stood. "So all guests know about the carpets?"

"Yes. They are told about them when they check in. They are even given a brochure marking where the magic carpets are located in various sheds around the resort."

Alex frowned. "Can you tell me a little more how it works?"

"You and your partner—if you have one—sit down on the carpet, and it instantly lifts you in the air. The rugs will take guests to the edge of our property line. And only that far. Part of the spell woven with the carpets was the fact they can only travel a specific distance. These rugs fly over the rocks my great-great-grandfather hauled in to the edge of the river...where my property stops. My grandparents thought it would be a great way for the guests to see the river, since the rocks kept them away." She stepped outside the building and pointed to another structure farther down the path. "That shed over there has magic carpets as well. Guests are free to ride them anywhere on our thirty acres—the river, the driving range and putting area, and even to the large pond." She pointed to another area, but all I could make out was the roof. "Way down there, we have the pond and boat rides. If guests don't want to get in the pond, they can take the magic carpet out and just sit and watch others play on the water."

We stepped back inside the building.

"So these carpets," Alex said, "fly over the rocks and stop at the edge of the embankment that leads to the river?"

"Yes. Allowing guests to sit and watch the river."

I caught Alex's eyes, and I knew he was thinking what I was. It also allowed a guest to dump a body off the carpet, causing the body to roll down the embankment and enter the churning river. Which is exactly what I surmised happened. Only instead of continuing downstream, Nate's clothing got snagged on the branches of the fallen tree and kept him anchored.

Alex sighed. "So this shed could potentially be an extension of our crime scene. I'm afraid I'm going to have to close this structure with the magic carpets down."

Melody's chin trembled, but she nodded. "I understand. I just can't believe this has happened."

"Can I talk with you a minute?" I asked Alex.

Melody took out her walkie-talkie. "I need to check in at the hotel. I'll just step outside and give you two some privacy."

"Thank you," Alex said. "Oh, and Melody?"

She turned around. "Yes?"

"No one goes into Nate's room until we've examined it."

Melody nodded. "Of course." She cleared her throat. "We only gave out one key to that room. Nate should have had it."

Alex nodded. "We found a key, along with his wallet, in his pants. They're in evidence."

Melody shook her head. "So sad. Then that should be the only one out. We can make you a new one. I'll have Harper rope off Nate's door."

I waited for her to leave before turning to Alex.

"I saw some dark stains on one of the carpets. Possibly blood." I looped my arm through a strap and dropped my backpack. "I have a way of preserving samples. Want me to scrape?"

"Please."

I took out the items I needed, scraped the sample, then stuffed it inside my backpack. "You realize there's not near enough blood on this carpet for a murder to have taken place. Especially one where the victim was stabbed through the heart."

"Yep. Which means we have *another* potential crime scene to find," Alex mused. "What did the killer do? Stab Nate near here, wait until the body stopped bleeding so much, drag him on the magic carpet, and then when they got to the edge of the river's embankment, just dumped the body over?"

"That's exactly what I'm thinking," I said. "So how do we find the other crime scene?"

Alex sighed. "Good question."

We walked back outside, and Melody met us halfway. "I'm having Harper come back down with rope and a sign stating the structure is closed down until further notice."

"Thank you," Alex said.

"Princess! Princess!"

Needles stopped in front of my face, his wings shimmering greenish-blue and fluttering a mile a minute. *"Come quick. I think I found something. The trees were upset, and now I know why."*

We took off jogging after Needles, who led us back to where we'd first met Melody. Alex had Melody stay put as we crossed the sidewalk and pushed our way through a tangle of shrubs and trees off the beaten path and into the woods.

"I think this is where the boy was killed," Needles said.

Sure enough, a pool of congealed blood was visible on the forest floor.

"Nice work, Needles," I said. "Looks like we have our original crime scene. Now to find the killer."

Chapter Five

Two hours later, we were finally making the ten-minute walk up the cement pathway to The Spellmoore. Alex and I had processed each crime scene together, and since Grant was still with the Howlers, Alex had Deputy Sparks rope off both the shed and the forested area with official crime scene tape. When we finished, Sparks left with the evidence to give to Finn Faeton, the undisputed queen of the forensics lab.

We entered the hotel from the back. The spacious patio had ten wrought-iron tables and chairs that overlooked a small pond with live ducks and a water fountain in the middle. As I walked over the cobblestone floor, I winced at the thought of what my muddy shoes would do to the interior floor of the hotel.

Alex held open one of the glass double doors, and I stepped inside.

"Welcome back. I hope your outing was delightful."

Alex and I both stared openmouthed at the enchanted table just inside the door. The enchanted *talking* table.

"That's so weird," Alex said as we continued walking.

"But cool," I said.

Sofas and chairs in various heights and colors were clustered around the middle of the room. To the left was a dark gray and white marble fireplace that took up nearly the entire wall. It wasn't on, but a man and woman sat in the wingback chairs in front of the hearth, laughing and talking. Along the other wall was a game area where a few guests sat playing checkers and chess.

"Fancy place," Needles said from his perch on my shoulder. *"Maybe you should enchant some of your furniture, Princess."*

"Never in a million years," I said.

"What?" Alex asked.

"Oh, Needles thought maybe I should enchant some of my furniture at the castle."

Alex winced. "Please don't."

We continued straight ahead and entered the lobby. To my right was a curved, gray and white marble staircase that led to the second floor. The tile floor was white with thin streaks of gray, and a Persian rug—like the magic carpets outside—took up a large section of the room.

"Good afternoon," a woman said from behind a marble counter. "I'm the concierge, Bellamy Pinetree. Ms. Spellmoore told me to ring her immediately when you made your way up to the hotel. Just one second, please."

A few minutes later, Melody Spellmoore hurried out from a door across the hall. The shaky smile on her face didn't reach her eyes. "Hello, again. Um, I'm not sure where you want to start. Maybe questioning Jordan?" She held up her hands. "I haven't told him anything, of course. In fact, I haven't seen him around at all."

"Actually," Alex said, "we'd like to see Nate's room first."

"Of course." She hurried back around the counter, typed something on the computer, then ran an electronic keycard through a device. "Here you go." She handed the key to Alex. "Room 208. His business partner, Jordan Owlman, is right across the hall in 209." Her voice cracked, and she blinked back tears. "I'm so sorry. I just can't believe this has happened. And I know I keep saying that, but it's true. We've *never* had an issue in all the time The Spellmoore has been open, much less something as horrific as this. This kind of thing isn't supposed to happen on Enchanted Island."

We stepped onto the elevator and made the short ride to the second floor in silence. When the doors opened, an upholstered bench with tons of tassels came to attention from across the hall.

"Watch your step, please." His tassels shook as he spoke. "We hope you enjoy your stay at The Spellmoore."

I chuckled. "I'm loving the enchanted furniture more and more."

When we reached Nate's room, I waited for Alex to swipe the card over the scanner, then stepped inside the spacious room and into the foyer. A half-table pushed against the wall held fresh flowers and a long oval bowl. A wadded up piece of paper lay inside the bowl.

"Let me," I said.

Waving my hand, I levitated the paper out of the bowl and magically straightened it midair so we could read what it said.

"Showoff," Alex chuckled.

I grinned. "Pretty much." I leaned forward and read. "Meet me where the sidewalk ends near the rocks and magic carpet shed. It's an emergency."

"Well, we know why Nate was down in that area," Alex said. "Now we just need to find out who left him the note."

"I'm not sure the fact the note is written on the hotel's letterhead is really a clue. All of our suspects are staying here, or in Anya's case has access to the hotel."

I retrieved an evidence bag from my backpack and used my magic to get it inside. I didn't want to touch any part of the paper just in case there might be prints on it outside of Nate's.

We walked down a short hallway and entered the great room. Directly in front of us, a set of French doors led to a small balcony that overlooked the back patio and small pond with the ducks and statue I saw earlier. There was a living room in the middle, a kitchenette to the right, and to the left of the living room was an office area complete with desk and chair. To the left of that was another set of French doors. A large king-sized bed was the only thing I could see. I assumed there was an en suite bathroom as well.

"I'll check his bedroom," Alex said. "You poke around the desk and see if there's anything important lying around."

"And what exactly are we looking for?" I asked.

"Anything out of the ordinary. A threatening note. Anything that might give us an idea who would be so mad at this guy that they'd lure him down to the river's edge and stab him in the heart."

Once again, I used my magic to rifle through the papers on Nate's desk. There were three separate thick packs of stapled paper with graphs and charts and verbiage about the app, and on each paper it looked like Nate wrote notes in the margin. Some had pros and some had cons. But nothing was written in a way that led me to believe if a competitor saw the notes that they'd be angry enough to kill Nate.

"I didn't really see anything," Alex said. "How about you?"

I shook my head. "Nope."

"I found a bag of opened pretzels," Needles said as he flew over to me. *"I ate a couple."*

"This is a potential crime scene," I said.

"What?" he lifted his paws in the air and shrugged. *"I was hungry."*

Chapter Six

"I understand what Melody was saying earlier downstairs," I said as we crossed the hall to Jordan Owlman's room. "Do you know why I left the island and joined the paranormal police department when I was just eighteen?"

"No," Alex said. "Why?"

"Because it was the most exciting thing I could think of. Melody is right. Nothing really exciting—or bad—ever happened here. I know we've learned lately that there have been rogue supernaturals down through the ages…but for the most part, the island was safe. And safe meant boring to me."

"How do you feel now?" Alex asked.

I knocked on Jordan's door. "Overwhelmed. Sad that the island has changed."

"Black Forest King feels the same way," Needles said. *"He, too, is upset by the slow changes he has witnessed."*

The door opened, and a disheveled-looking man in his mid-twenties answered the door. His hair stuck out haphazardly from his head—like it had a mind of its own. The clothes on his tall, lean frame looked like they'd never seen an iron or a dryer, but something about the way he shoved his large oval glasses up his nose was endearing.

Definitely an owl shifter.

"Jordan Owlman?" Alex asked.

"Yes." He leaned forward and stared at Needles. "Is that a porcupine with wings?"

I breathed a sigh of relief. Usually people asked if Needles was a hedgehog, and I had to listen to him rant about the differences between the two species. "Yes. He's my—my pet."

I knew that would piss Needles off, but I also didn't feel comfortable as a forty-year-old witch introducing him as my bodyguard.

"You need to tell people I'm your partner," Needles said. *"Pet is gonna get you coal for Yule. Just a little warning."*

I bit back a smile at the threat.

"Fascinating." Jordan stepped back. "Come in, come in. Please. Thank you for coming. I keep trying to call Nate's phone, but it just goes to his voicemail. It's not like Nate to miss a meeting."

Alex held up his hand. "Why don't we all sit down."

"Oh, right." Jordan ran his hands through his hair. "I just don't know what to do. On top of Nate not answering his phone, I also keep getting phone calls from our three potential buyers. Nate and I were supposed to make a decision today about who we were going with."

He led us down the hallway and into the great room. It was the same room Nate had, just flipped. Jordan had his French doors open, letting in the breeze.

"This is a lovely room," I said as Alex and I sat down on the sofa across from Jordan. "I had no idea The Spellmoore was so extravagant."

Jordan sighed. "It wasn't my idea to stay here, but then Nate reminded me the rooms could be written off on our taxes, and so I said yes." He wiped his hands on his jeans. "You think this is extravagant, you should see the penthouse suites. This is just the second floor. These have balconies, kitchenettes, and one bedroom. The penthouse suites on the third floor have two bedrooms, a kitchenette, and a larger balcony."

"You two didn't want to room together and do the penthouse?" I asked.

Jordan shook his head. "No. I like my space. Nate and I live together, and it can sometimes get cramped when his girlfriend comes over. This is a stressful enough time for our business. I didn't need Anya adding to the stress."

"Let's start at the beginning," Alex said. "My name is Sheriff Stone, and this is Agent Loci. I'm afraid I have some bad news about Nate Howler."

"Bad news? No. This is an exciting time for us." He closed his eyes, and his chin trembled. "Please don't tell me bad news."

"I'm afraid Nate's body was discovered earlier today in the river," Alex said. "He's dead."

"No!" Jordan stood up and paced. "No. I don't believe it. Nate was an excellent swimmer. Besides, why would he be at the river?" He stopped. "Wait. The river or the pond where the boats are? Because if you mean the river where the cutoff is to the north side of the island, I'm going to tell you no way." He glanced nervously at me. "I know who you are. The rumors have made the rounds since you came back to live here. Nate and I were raised on the island. We *know* not to go to the river." He swallowed hard and shook his head. "No way would Nate go there."

"I'm the one who discovered his body," I said as gently as I could. "I'm sorry to tell you it's true."

On a sob, Jordan stepped back over to his chair and dropped. "It doesn't make any sense."

"I'm curious," I said. "Whose idea was it for you two to stay here instead of driving home each night?"

Jordan looked up, his big owl-like eyes blinking at me. He finally gave himself a little shake and sat up straight. "Nate thought it would be best if we all stayed clustered together. You know, in case our buyers had questions."

"Why don't you start there," Alex said. "What buyers?"

"Oh, right. Sorry." Jordan cleared his throat. "See, Nate and I are in the middle of negotiations. We have three companies competing for our app."

"Your app?" Alex mused.

"Yes. Nate and I developed a dating app called Super Single." He chuckled and slid his glasses back up his nose. "Get it? It's a dating app for supernatural singles. We've brought it along as far as we can with our limited resources, and now we'd like to sell. We have three big-name companies wanting it. So they agreed to fly to Enchanted Island and pitch their proposals to us for the app, and then we were going to choose which company we wanted to sell to."

"So these three companies are still here?" Alex asked.

"Yes. Well, not their entire companies, of course. Just the person they sent to close the deal."

"I take it the closers are all supernatural?" I asked.

"Oh, yes." He lifted both hands in the air, his eyes wide with fear. "We wouldn't dare sell to a non-supernatural company. We know better."

Alex withdrew his notepad. "We're going to need the names of the three closers you are working with."

Jordan nodded. "Of course. Gracie Pixman, Mavis Firestone, and Owen Oldblood."

"And just so we're aware," Alex said, "because I definitely don't know the answer...what kind of money are we talking? What are these companies willing to pay to buy this app?"

Jordan cleared his throat. "About three hundred thousand dollars."

"Seriously?" I asked. "That's big money."

"And a big motive to kill," Needles said.

"You arrived here at the resort on Tuesday?" Alex mused. "Is that correct?"

Jordan frowned. "Yes. How did you know?"

"We've spoken to Melody Spellmoore," I said. "The owner of the resort."

Jordan shook his head. "Right. I'm sorry. I'm not usually so slow on the uptake. It's like I'm in a fog or something."

"You're doing fine," I said.

Needles lifted off my shoulder and hovered in the air. *"I'm going to see what I can discover outside."*

He shot out the open French doors and was gone in the blink of an eye.

"Everything okay?" Alex asked.

"Yeah," I said. "He's just going to investigate."

"That blows my mind," Jordan said.

"So you arrived on Tuesday?" Alex prompted.

"Right. Nate and I arrived Tuesday morning, got settled in. Around two, we met in the conference room downstairs on the first floor and went over our presentation to the three potential buyers. Afterward, we all left and did our own thing. I believe Alex had drinks later that evening with the potential buyers."

"You didn't?" I asked.

Jordan shook his head. "Not really my thing. I came back up here after the two o'clock meeting and worked on a couple projects we're thinking of starting once we sell to—" He broke off as tears filled his eyes. "I guess we won't be doing that now."

"What about yesterday?" Alex asked, once Jordan had himself under control. "How did your schedule look?"

"There was a lot of downtime, so I know Nate was doing the thing he does—did best. Which is schmoozing the clients. So I think I remember him saying he was going to take in the resort sights with different buyers midmorning. You'd have to ask them." He wiped his hands on his jeans. "Around two, Nate and I started our last of the meetings. This time, each person gave us their pitch individually. So we had a two o'clock, a four o'clock, and a six o'clock. Then Nate was having a late dinner with his girlfriend. After that, I think he told me he was doing drinks again with the buyers." He shrugged. "I really don't know anything more than that. Nate and I agreed to meet up this morning around ten to go over everything we'd heard from each pitch, and then we were going to make a joint decision and reveal the winning company around two o'clock." A tear slid down his cheek under his glasses. "But I guess that's not happening, either."

Alex waited a minute for Jordan to collect himself. "Do you know anyone who would want to hurt Nate?"

"No. Everyone loved him. I mean that. It's not just something I'm saying. That's why Nate was the face of our company." Jordan sighed. "I write the code, and he brings in the business. That was our deal. Nate has this—had this way of bringing people together and making them feel important. He was charismatic, you know? Everyone wanted to be around him. Heck, myself included. We've been friends since elementary school." He wiped at another tear that fell under his glasses. "I'm really going to miss him."

"How did you two meet?" I asked.

Jordan chuckled. "The typical jock and nerd way. We were in fifth grade, and a couple werewolf boys started pushing me around on the playground. Nate stepped in, and that was it. Nate was a werewolf shifter too. I mean, I guess you already know that. Anyway, he was big and strong and good at all the things I wasn't." Jordan turned his gaze to the wall and was silent for a few seconds. "I'm an owl shifter. I'm not any of those things. But Nate didn't care. When I talked books and nerd stuff, he just nodded and listened. It was...the most amazing thing I'd ever experienced. And I thought it would end as we got older, you know? I mean, he was *really* popular, and I wasn't. But it was never like that between us."

"He sounds like a great friend," I said.

Jordan nodded. "He was. Nate tried taking me to parties and on double dates with him in high school, but it wasn't for me. And we still remained friends. We decided to go to Super U—an all supernatural university up in Maine. Nate majored in business, and I majored in computers. We lived in the dorms our freshman year, and then rented a house until graduation. After we graduated, we came back to Enchanted Island. It's where our families live, and it's where we knew we wanted to run our business from."

"That's admirable," I said.

Jordan's face crumbled, and he buried his face in his hands and wept. I looked away and brushed aside a couple of my own tears. I heard Alex get up and return a few seconds later, setting a box of tissue down on the coffee table. After a few minutes, Jordan lifted his head, grabbed a tissue, and wiped his face.

Needles chose that moment to fly back inside the room and land on my shoulder. *"Miss anything, Princess?"*

I shook my head.

"I'm sorry." Jordan blew his nose. "I'm just gutted by all this."

"I understand," Alex said. "Can you answer a few more questions for us?"

Jordan nodded.

Alex clicked his pen. "So you're telling us you can't think of anyone who would want to hurt Nate?"

Jordan shook his head. "No. I mean, he and his girlfriend, Anya, are sort of on the outs right now, I think. But I can't imagine Anya physically hurting Nate."

"My money's on her," Needles said. *"It's always the jilted lover."*

I bit my lip to keep from laughing.

"Why were they fighting?" Alex asked.

Jordan sighed. "Like I said, Nate was the face of the company. On top of being charismatic, he was good looking. So he became the guinea pig for the company."

"Why guinea pig?" Needles asked. *"Why not cat or cow?"*

"Stop," I hissed out of the corner of my mouth.

"We took out an ad in the Enchanted Island newspaper," Jordan continued, "asking women aged twenty-one to thirty to download our app and fill it out. Our app suggested the two women Nate had the most in common with, and he went out with the two potential dates. Anya knew it was only for business purposes, but she didn't like it." He sighed. "And then when Super Solutions sent Gracie Pixman to the island to close the deal for their company, that *really* sent Anya over the edge."

"Why's that?" I asked.

"Gracie and Nate used to date in high school before she moved away."

"Yep. Get out the binder. It's Anya." Needles' wings shimmered green. *"Jealousy. Gets ya every time."*

"What's Anya's last name?" Alex asked.

"Moony. Anya Moony. She's a werewolf shifter like Nate. We all went to school together, but Anya stayed on the island and got a job at EI Athletics while Nate and I went to college. When we came back, Nate hooked up with Anya. They're a pretty serious item. I mean, until recently."

"EI Athletics?" Alex mused. "You mean the store that sells camping, hiking, and all that outdoorsy equipment stuff?"

Jordan nodded. "Yes. She's a floor manager."

"Where does Anya live?" Alex asked.

"In a rental on Ghost Pine Drive."

Alex pointed to my backpack on the floor, and I leaned over and withdrew the crumpled note and handed it to Jordan.

"Have you ever seen this?" I asked.

Jordan frowned as he read it. "No. Was this in Nate's room or something? Is this why he was down by the river?" He flipped the baggie over but nothing was written on the back side of the paper. "I don't recognize the handwriting. In fact, I'd say they went out of their way to disguise the handwriting. It looks deliberately stilted in some areas."

I took the bag from him and glanced down at the paper. He was right. Now that I looked at it again, it *did* look choppy in some places.

"I have to ask, Jordan," Alex said gently. "Where were you last night between ten and four this morning?"

Jordan's eyes widened. "Here. I stayed in my room. I never left it. I swear." He gestured to the desk. "I worked on our idea for a new application."

Alex stood. "I think that's all I need for right now. Again, we're sorry for your loss."

"Thank you."

Alex and I headed toward the door.

"One last question," Alex said, turning to face Jordan. "What happens now?"

Jordan frowned. "What do you mean?"

"To the company?" Alex clarified. "What will happen to the company? Who will get Nate's half of the company?"

Jordan blinked a couple times, his big, owl-like eyes just staring. "Well, I guess I do."

Chapter Seven

We made our way back to the lobby and motioned Melody over.

"We'd like to see the kitchen," Alex said. "I want to know where the knife was located."

"Of course." Melody placed her hands on her stomach. "I'm sorry if I keep stumbling over myself."

I laid my hand on her arm. "It's okay, Melody. Sheriff Stone and I are just looking for answers, that's all."

"I know." She took a deep breath, then exhaled. "The restaurant is down this hallway here. If you'll follow me."

We took a left and followed her down the hallway.

"Pretty bottles!" Needles sprang off my shoulder and flew back and forth across the narrow hall, looking at the empty, dusty bottles that sat on shelves behind glass encasements.

"Oh! He startled me." Melody stopped and watched Needles zip around the hallway, hovering in the air and taking in the bottles. "These are all the liquor bottles from the bar that we've collected over the years. Some of them date back as far as the eighteen hundreds."

"Amazing," I said. "A unique collection of history."

"I've always thought the same thing," Melody said as she continued down the hall. "Some families have art or jewelry they pass down from generation to generation. My family passed down booze bottles." She giggled. "Wonder what that says about us?" She pushed open a set of swinging doors as Needles landed back on my shoulder. "This is the lounge or bar area."

The room was dimly lit, and since it was still afternoon, not many guests sat on the stools or in the surrounding booths and tables. I nodded to the woman behind the bar as Melody continued walking through the lounge and into another room.

"It's lovely," I whispered.

This room was in stark contrast to the darkened bar. This spacious room was basically a greenhouse. Not only were the three walls floor-to-ceiling glass, but so was the ceiling itself. Dozens of potted plants hung from the rafters.

"Thank you. This is our restaurant." She pushed through another set of swinging door. "And back here is the kitchen."

It was set up like a tradition restaurant kitchen with different station groupings. Unlike the bar, this area was a beehive of activity. Servers were rushing in and out the door setting up tables, and chefs and cooks were busy prepping for the evening meal.

"Drake, one of our kitchen stewards, was the first to notice the carving knife was missing," Melody said. "After an extensive search, he came to me this morning to let me know."

"Is Drake still here?" Alex asked.

"Yes. I asked him to stay late so he could speak with you. Drake usually works breakfast and lunch." Melody led us to another room. "This is where we wash and dry dishes."

Two men and one woman looked up when we walked into the room. I could hear the hum of the commercial-grade dishwasher running through its cycle. One of the men stood in front of a sink and rinsed off dirty dishes, then stacked them next to the dishwasher. The woman was wiping off the countertops, while the other man wrote in a notebook.

"Drake," Melody said, "the police would like to talk to you."

The young man stopped rinsing the plate, wiped his hands on his apron, then walked over to where we stood. He had short, spikey hair, a round baby face, and barely looked old enough to drive. "I thought I'd wash off a few dishes while I waited. I'd offer you my hand, but it might not be very clean."

"It's okay," Alex said. "What is your full name?"

He swallowed hard, and his Adam's apple bobbed up and down. "Drake. Drake Catman."

"Panther shifter?" I mused.

Drake shook his head. "I'm a Normal, ma'am."

Norm or Normal was the term used to describe those who, despite having supernatural parents, couldn't shift or didn't have any magical abilities.

Alex nodded. "Okay. When did you notice the carving knife was missing?"

"I'm in charge of making sure the chefs have the cutlery they need," Drake said. "I usually work mornings, so I come in and set out what each chef will need beforehand. Because we serve ham and other meats for breakfast, I know I need to set out the carving knife. Only this morning, it wasn't where it was supposed to be. I called the Chief Steward, Philby, who always closes except on his two nights off, and he said he put it back where it was supposed to go last night."

"Okay," Alex said. "And what time does Philby usually close down the kitchen? Do you know?"

Drake glanced at Melody. "I might be wrong, but I think he's usually done by ten-thirty. The kitchen stops serving at nine during the weekday, so they finish up back here around ten-thirty."

"That's about right," Melody said. "The kitchen stays open until eleven on Friday and Saturday, but during the week everyone is usually gone by ten-thirty."

I glanced around the room and noticed the other two workers listening in. "Where was the knife supposed to be located?"

Drake pointed to a row of knives hanging from a magnetic knife rack. Each knife was encased in a see-through bag. "Makes for easy grab-and-go."

"Who has access to this part of the kitchen?" Alex asked.

"Pretty much everyone," Drake said.

A door next to the sink opened, and a teenager strolled in from outside, whistling a snappy tune. He stopped when he saw us. "Uh…sorry. Can I come in?"

"How did you enter through that door?" Alex asked. "Do you have a key? Was it locked?"

I put my hand out to stop the door from closing. "Kitchen Staff Only" was clearly marked on the door from the outside. Anyone passing by would see it.

The boy shook his head, his mop of hair moving on its own. "Nah. It's how the kitchen staff normally comes in because that's our parking lot." His brows furrowed. "Did I do something wrong?"

"No," Alex said. "I was just wondering if that door is locked at night."

The young man shrugged. "I've never known it to be."

"Thank you," Alex said. "You can go on."

The boy hurried out of the room, and the man who had been writing in the notebook stepped forward. "He's right. My name's

Zane, and no one really locks it. I mean, we've never had a reason *to* lock it. No one has ever messed with our stuff. I've been here five years, and never once heard of anything being stolen."

"I'll rectify this immediately," Melody said.

Chapter Eight

I stood in front of The Spellmoore with Needles perched on my shoulder, as Alex wrapped up his call to Zoie. It was going on four o'clock, and he didn't want her to worry when he wasn't home for dinner. I knew she was still wrestling with the fact she was half witch and half gargoyle—that last part only being revealed to her a few weeks ago.

"She's good," Alex said, bringing me back to the present. "I think I'll call Grant and have him drive by Ghost Pine Drive and talk with—"

The squealing of tires stopped Alex's words. A girl in an old Jeep leaped out of the driver's side and looked wildly around. "Hello? Hello?"

Two valets ran toward her, and Alex and I moved as one to see what was going on.

"I demand answers," the girl said. "I heard over the police scanner that the sheriff and—" She broke off when she saw us. "Omigosh! Is it Nate? Is it?"

Alex and I looked at each other as the girl covered her face and started to cry.

"Keep her away from me," Needles said, disgust evident in his voice. *"I don't want her snotting all over my wings."*

"I bet that's Anya Moony," I whispered. "No sense sending Grant over to her house to speak with her."

Alex gave me a small smile. "Let's find out."

When we stopped in front of the crying girl, she lifted her head but continued to let the tears fall. I placed her at mid-twenties, long brunette hair, brown eyes, and square jaw. She finally swiped at her tears, and I couldn't help but be impressed by the muscles in her arms. Something about her said she could hold her own in a fistfight.

"I've been trying to reach Nate all day," she said. "I've called his cell about twenty times, and I even called Jordan a few hours ago, but he hadn't heard from Nate either. I know something is wrong."

"You must be Anya Moony," Alex said.

The girl gasped. "You've spoken with Nate? Where is he? Why wouldn't he return my calls? He knows how I worry."

I put my hand on Anya's arm. "Anya, my name is Shayla Loci, and this is Sheriff Stone. I'm afraid we have some bad news. Nate Howler is dead."

She took a step back, her head shaking vigorously. "You're wrong. There must be some mistake."

"I'm afraid not," I said. "His parents have already been notified."

She bent over as though punched in the gut. "Dead? How? He seemed fine last night. Did he get sick?"

"Cause of death is still out," Alex said. "Ms. Moony, we've spoken to a couple different people who have mentioned you were having problems in your relationship with Nate. Can you tell me about that?"

Anya straightened and narrowed her eyes at Alex. "*Excuse me?* Nate and I weren't fighting. Whoever told you that is mistaken. We weren't fighting. Nate *loved* me."

Needles flew off my shoulder and did a flip in the air. *"Is she convincing us or herself? I think she's a little liar."* His wings shimmered yellow, and he emitted a high-pitched laugh. *"Is her nose growing, Princess?"*

I widened my eyes at him so he'd be quiet and stop trying to make me laugh. Which only tickled Needles more.

Alex must have realized what was going on, because he glared at Needles and cleared his throat. "We've been told not only were you fighting with Nate Howler, but you'd also had words with Gracie Pixman, one of the potential buyers for the Super Single app. Are you saying that's not true?"

"Nate *loved* me. After he made this big sell, we were going to move into our own place together. He was going to move out of Jordan's place and *we'd* start being a couple." She snorted. "Jordan probably didn't tell you that, did he? Or the fact now that Nate is—" She broke off into sobs, and we let her cry for a couple seconds. When she pulled herself together, she wiped her face and looked up, her eyes fierce and angry. "Did Jordan tell you with Nate dead that *he* has control of the company now?"

"That was mentioned," Alex said.

"Ha!" Anya's arms flew wildly in the air. "That should be proof enough Jordan killed my one true love." She frowned. "Or that tart Gracie Pixman did. She's been trying to get her hooks into Nate all week. You need to arrest her." She gasped and clasped her hands to her head. "Maybe they *both* plotted to kill Nate! I bet that's it! You need to arrest them *both*."

"That's actually not how this works," Alex said. "Agent Loci and I will continue to question everyone involved, gather evidence, and proceed from there. If you can give me your phone number and address in case we have more questions for you later, that would be helpful."

"I'm not leaving here," Anya said. "I'm getting a room and staying right here until I know for sure what happened to Nate. I'll find out which one of these monsters killed him."

"She's gonna be trouble," Needles said in a sing-song voice.

I nodded in agreement, but didn't voice it aloud.

"Actually, Ms. Moony," Alex said coldly, "you will do no such thing. If you attempt to butt into our investigation, I *will* have you arrested. Are we clear about that?"

Tears welled in her eyes. "But they killed my beautiful Nate."

"I changed my mind," Needles said. *"I kinda like her now. She's so melodramatic...she'll be a hoot to watch. I should have popcorn during this investigation. Then, every time I see her, I'll pull it out and munch on it."*

I let out a bark of laughter. I couldn't help myself. I'd mentally pictured Needles munching popcorn and acting like a nosy teenaged girl, and it made me laugh.

"It's not funny," Anya said.

"You're right," I said. "I apologize. My laughter had nothing to do with you or what you'd said."

Anya narrowed her eyes at Needles, who'd gone back to perching on my shoulder. "What is that?"

"My associate," I said.

"Oh, nice. Your associate." He laughed. *"I like it."*

"Ms. Moony," Alex said, "can you tell me where you were last night from six in the evening to six in the morning?"

Her eyes went huge. "You think I had something to do with Nate's death? Does that mean his death wasn't natural? It does, doesn't it? So one of them *did* murder my lover."

Alex sighed. "Can you just answer the question without all the theatrics? It would really help us do our job."

Anya's mouth dropped. "Theatrics? Theatrics? The man I loved and planned on marrying and having kids with someday has been murdered, and you think I'm being *theatrical*?"

Alex held up his hand. "Do you want us to find out what happened to Nate?"

"Of course I do," Anya said. "That's a ridiculous question."

"Then do me a favor, and just answer *my* question. Where were you last night between six and six?"

I'd never really heard Alex lose his temper with a suspect before. In fact, it was rare for him to get angry at all. Sometimes he'd get snippy at Needles, but even that wasn't anger as much as exasperation.

Anya lifted her chin. "I arrived at The Spellmoore around eight for dinner with Nate. Afterward, he had drinks with the three people vying for his business."

I snorted. "You mean the business Nate and Jordan co-own?"

I couldn't help myself.

Anya huffed. "Yes, that business. Although, why they were fifty-fifty partners, I don't know. Jordan just designed and got the app to work. It was Nate's hard work that brought recognition to the app and who finally enlisted three companies to compete for his business."

I didn't ask her if part of Nate's hard work consisted of him dating other women…I figured I'd already upset the apple cart enough for one day.

"Your whereabouts, Ms. Moony?" Alex prompted wearily.

Anya sighed. "Like I said, Nate and I had a late dinner around eight. At nine, we met Gracie, Mavis, and Owen at the bar for a few drinks. Those are the three people hoping to get

Nate's app. I think I left around ten or ten-thirty, something like that. I went home and went to bed."

"Do you live alone?" I asked. "Or do you have a roommate? Live with your parents? Someone that could vouch for you and what time you got home?"

"I have a roommate," Anya said. "We work together, but she has a different set of friends. She's a fairy. Last night, she was still out when I got home. I have no idea what time she got in. I heard her getting coffee in the kitchen around seven this morning."

I frowned. "So she couldn't confirm you were home by ten-thirty?"

"I guess not. But I didn't kill Nate."

Alex nodded to me. "Agent Loci is going to show you a note, Ms. Moony. Can you tell me if you've ever seen it before?"

I slid the backpack off my shoulders, reached in and grabbed the evidence bag, then handed it to her. She quickly scanned it, then thrust it back at me.

"I have no idea what this is about," she said, "but it just proves someone wanted to hurt my Nate. Which is why I'm sticking around until someone gets arrested."

Alex sighed. "I guess I can't stop you from staying here. Go check and see if they have an extra room for you, then let us know which room you're in."

"They should have rooms left," Anya said. "That's why Nate chose this week. There wasn't a wedding or anything else going on out here, and so the resort wasn't full."

At that, my head jerked up. Just last night over dinner, Serena had been going on and on about not having a place to hold her and Grant's wedding. I'd almost offered my castle to her, but I really didn't want a lot of townspeople traipsing around so close to Black Forest. I don't know why neither of us thought of this place. With our own houses on the island, there was never a need to vacation at The Spellmoore. But having the wedding here made perfect sense.

"I think I'm going to do the same," I said as Anya hurried inside the hotel.

"What?" Alex asked.

"What? Why?" Needles demanded. *"We have our own lair to lay our heads. A nice comfy castle. Remember, Princess?"*

"Serena has been looking for a venue for her wedding," I said, ignoring Needles. "This is the perfect place. I think I'm going to call her and have her stay out here with me for a day or two."

"What about my things?" Needles demanded. *"I need my toothbrush and pajamas."*

I rolled my eyes at him. "Stop worrying, Needles. After we question the three potential buyers, I'll drive us home and pack a bag and meet Serena back here. It's the perfect plan."

"And while you're here," Alex said, "you can do some more digging."

I grinned. "Exactly. Talk to employees, bartenders, that kind of thing."

"I like it," Alex said. "You call Serena, and I'll see about our three persons of interest."

Chapter Nine

"Serena said she'd be here around eight," I said when Alex joined Needles and me outside at a table overlooking the small pond out back. "I rented us a room for two nights."

"Great. I heard from Grant. He said the parents were understandably distraught. They couldn't imagine someone wanting to hurt Nate. Everyone loved him. Same thing we've heard about him. I asked Grant to run background checks on Jordan Owlman, Anya Moony, and the three buyers just to start us off."

"Smart. There's big money at stake here," I said. "Any of the three competing companies would have a motive. I'm sure each one wants to snag the Super Single app. With Nate being the face of the company, if they eliminate him, then that just leaves Jordan. And we've met Jordan. No way is he a ruthless negotiator. One of those three—whoever the killer was—could swoop in and undermine the others and get Jordan to sell to them."

"I'll agree," Alex said, "but that's a lot of risk for not a lot to show for."

"Unless keeping their job depended on getting the deal," I said.

"True. But Jordan has the highest motive I can think of right now. He admitted with Nate's death he'll have one hundred percent controlling interest in the company."

"True," I agreed. "Although we can't dismiss Anya Moony. Jealousy is always a motive for murder. Not only would that kind of big money change Nate's and Jordan's personal lives, but we've heard from two people that Anya was argumentative while at The Spellmoore, and she didn't like Nate testing out the online dating app, *and* with the ex-girlfriend back in town…I definitely say Anya needs to be on the suspect list."

Alex grinned. "I think I remember a song a few years back about crazy ex-girlfriends."

I winked at him. "We exist."

Needles snorted. *"If this is your idea of flirting, you're gonna be single forever."*

"Shut up," I mumbled.

Alex raised an eyebrow. "Needles?"

"Always," I said.

Needles laughed, sprang off my shoulder, and did a twirl in the air. *"Just trying to help your love life, Princess."*

I was about to respond when a mid-twenties blonde dressed in a red designer pantsuit and sporting giant sunglasses pushed through the glass door and looked around. When she spotted us, she headed our way.

"Behave," I said to Needles.

"Hello." Her voice was soft and gentle. "My name's Gracie Pixman."

Alex stood and motioned for her to sit across from us. "Thank you for meeting with us, Ms. Pixman. My name's Sheriff

Stone, and this is my partner, Agent Loci. I'm sorry for your loss."

Gracie slid her sunglasses off and set them on the table in front of her, giving me a clear view of her puffy, red-swollen eyes. "I still can't believe Nate is dead."

I could hear the pain in her voice. "I'm sorry."

She smiled fleetingly. "Thank you. Yet 'sorry' just doesn't seem to do the pain justice."

Because she was right, I let the comment go.

"I understand you are here at The Spellmoore on business," Alex said. "Your company would like to acquire the app that Jordan and Nate have developed? Is that about right?"

Gracie nodded. "Basically."

"When we spoke to Jordan," Alex continued, "he indicated the competing companies were willing to pay large amounts of money for the application."

Again Gracie nodded. "Standard, really. It's an amazing app Nate and Jordan came up with. Wonderful idea. Unfortunately, they've taken it as far as they can on their limited resources. By my company acquiring the rights to the application, we can take it where they only dreamed of going."

"So a big deal for Nate and Jordan," Alex said, "and for the company that gains the rights?"

Gracie nodded. "Yes. And I know where you're going with this, Sheriff. I doubt any of us murdered Nate because he wouldn't choose our company."

"I never said Nate was murdered," Alex said. "We're still waiting on cause of death."

Gracie snorted and wiped at a tear. "I watch cop shows on TV, Sheriff. I know how this kind of thing works."

I pretended to cough in order to hide my smile. It was the

snippiest thing Gracie had said so far, and the funniest. "Your bracelet is beautiful."

And it was. Every time she moved her delicate hand, the diamonds glittered.

"Thank you." Gracie ran a finger over the top. "A gift from my mother and father when I graduated college. I never take it off."

"Speaking of them," I said. "I understand you grew up on the island."

She nodded. "Until my junior year. Then Dad got a job with a supernatural pharmaceutical company, and we moved away."

"So you know the island pretty well?" I mused.

Gracie shrugged. "I guess."

I shifted in my seat so I could look her in the eyes. "You'd know not to try and cross the river and go to the north side of the island?"

Her mouth dropped. "Is that where Nate was found? I know the river runs along the back of The Spellmoore property because on our first day here, I took one of the magic carpets out to tour the resort."

"Let's talk about your arrival," Alex said. "You checked in Tuesday afternoon?"

"Yes. Around lunch. I grabbed a quick bite to eat, unpacked my clothes, then headed to the conference room a little before two for the boys to make their final pitch to us. After the meeting, I had a few hours to myself, so I took out a carpet. I saw the river and trees, watched some golfers for a while, and then went down to the pond where people were in paddle boats." She chuckled. "I even watched couples play tennis and pickleball."

"They have pickleball here?" I mused.

Gracie nodded. "They do." She shrugged. "I returned the magic carpet back where I got it, came back to my suite, then had dinner in my room. Nate informed us after the two o'clock meeting he'd like to meet the three of us—Mavis, Owen, and myself—in the bar around eight for drinks."

"Was Jordan at the bar?" Alex asked.

Gracie smiled. "No. I barely remember Jordan from high school. What I remember was that Nate and he were friends. Do you know what I mean? Jordan didn't do the social thing, unless Nate dragged him there." She chuckled. "And even when he attended, it was obvious Jordan was uncomfortable. But Nate always made sure Jordan was included."

"So you had drinks," Alex said. "Did anything relevant happen during that time?"

Gracie glanced up quickly and met Alex's gaze. "I assume you mean the confrontation Anya and I had in the restroom?"

"Enlighten me," Alex said.

"Everything was going great—at least for me. I won't lie. I was sent here by my company to close this deal because I had the best advantage. I was from the island, *and* I dated one of the potential sellers. We only broke up because my parents moved away, which meant we had no hard feelings." She shrugged. "So, yes, it was going well for me. Everyone was having a good time. Until Nate's girlfriend arrived. Anya Moony? I assume you've spoken with her?"

"Yes," Alex said. "Agent Loci and I spoke with her briefly."

Gracie shook her head, her long blonde hair cascading around her shoulders. "Isn't she something? Not at all what I pictured Nate with. I mean, she's—um, feisty?"

"Did she get feisty with you?" I asked.

Gracie smiled. "You can say that. Nate excused himself from the table to take a phone call, and the minute his back was turned, she came after me. With Mavis and Owen sitting right there! It was embarrassing and unprofessional. So I said I needed to use the restroom. I'd just gotten inside the bathroom when she barreled in behind me."

"What did she say?" I asked.

Gracie's cheeks turned pink, and even with her red blotchy eyes, she still looked pretty. "Accused me of trying to get Nate back. Told me if I didn't stop flirting with him in front of her—and I promise you, I wasn't—she'd knock a few of my pretty white teeth out, and she'd do whatever she had to do to make sure we don't end up together."

Alex shifted in his chair. "I don't suppose anyone overheard your argument in the bathroom?"

"Actually, yes." Gracie gave a short laugh. "That's what was so humiliating. It wasn't our server, but one of the servers working the other side of the bar. I don't know her name, but it was the most awkward thing ever. She flushed, opened the stall door, apologized, washed her hands as fast as she could, then bolted out the door. You might talk to her. She'll tell you how insane Anya seemed that night."

"What did you do after the server left?" Alex asked.

"I ran out of the bathroom behind her and went straight to my room." She closed her eyes, and a tear fell down her cheek. "I didn't want Nate back. I never did. And if my being here is what got him killed, I'll never be able to live with that."

Alex tapped his pen on the table. "Walk me through your day Wednesday."

"I was the first person to pitch to Nate and Jordan and have a chance to win the account," Gracie said. "I gave my presentation around two." She grinned. "It went great. Afterward, I went back to my room, called my boss to let him know how things were going, and then later, around four, I received a text from Nate saying he wanted to meet again for drinks around nine."

"I take it you went?" I asked.

"Of course." She sighed. "Although, had I known Anya was going to be there again, maybe I wouldn't have. I don't know. Anyway, I did my best not to even speak or look at Nate. Things were going well until Nate went to use the restroom. I decided I wouldn't sit at the table with Anya, even though Mavis and Owen were still there. I grabbed my purse and ran out of the bar."

"Did Anya follow you out of the bar?" I asked.

Gracie cleared her throat and shrugged. "If she did, I didn't see her."

Something about that didn't ring true. Maybe it was the way she averted her gaze, or the way she phrased the answer, but something seemed off.

"You want my opinion?" Gracie mused. "Anya did this. She killed Nate." She swiped at the tear rolling down her cheek, and the diamonds in her bracelet twinkled. "Anya somehow lured Nate out after we all left the bar Wednesday night and killed him. Maybe out of rage and jealousy? I don't know."

"What about the other two people you are competing against?" I asked. "Do you think one of them would want to hurt Nate?"

Gracie shrugged. "Maybe?" She blew out a deep breath. "I know for a fact if Owen doesn't get this account, his firm will fire him. He hasn't landed a new client in six months." She leaned back in her seat. "I have it on good authority from a friend of mine who has seen his resume go through her firm, that he's job hunting. He knows his time is up."

I frowned. "You seem pretty confident Owen wouldn't get this account."

Gracie smiled. "There was never a chance. Nate saw right through him. I take it you haven't met Owen yet?" She shuddered. "Owen tries to come off all charming and smooth. But really, he's just smarmy." She smiled. "Vampires. They think more of themselves than they should."

"True," Needles said, *"but not near as much as gargoyles do. One in particular."*

I turned my head and smiled. No way was I rising to that bait.

"Now," Gracie continued, "Mavis Firestone is another story. She's a shark in this business. Been doing it more years than I've been alive, I imagine." She giggled. "Well, maybe not. Definitely don't tell her I said that. She'd be mad."

I smiled. "Our lips are sealed."

"Anyway," Gracie said, "we are across the hall from each other, and on Tuesday afternoon, I was leaving my room as she was entering hers, so her back was to me. Well, she was on the phone, and I overheard her say that it wouldn't be the first time she'd gotten her hands dirty to snag a client. And then she laughed. A wicked laugh, if you know what I mean?"

"Shayla?" Alex mused. "Can you show Ms. Pixman the note we found?"

I reach in my backpack, withdrew the evidence bag containing the crumpled note, and slid it to her. "Do you recognize this note?"

Gracie read the note, shaking her head and frowning. "No. Doesn't look familiar to me."

I slid the note back to my side of the table. "Thank you."

Alex nodded. "Yes. Thank you for your time, Ms. Pixman. One last question. Where were you from eleven to four this morning?"

Gracie's hand shook as she picked up her sunglasses and shoved them back on her face. "I was in my hotel room sleeping. Alone."

Chapter Ten

"Something tells me all our interviews are going to go like this." I took a drink of the water the server had plunked down in front of Alex and me. "Mostly he said or she said and then a lot of wild speculation and throw in a so-and-so killed him."

Alex chuckled. "Probably. But even that may tell us something."

"What did you think of Gracie's story?" I asked.

"She didn't seem overly dramatic," Alex said with a smile, "which I appreciate."

"Plus, she's a looker," Needles said as he hovered in the air, wings shimmering gold, and walked in place…wiggling his backside the whole time.

Alex laughed. "I think I understand what Needles is saying."

I narrowed my eyes at Alex. "Is that so?"

Alex lifted one hand in surrender. "I didn't say anything." He pulled out his cell phone and shot off a text. "When you were still on the phone with Serena, I spoke to Melody. She volunteered to send out the three people we needed to speak to. All I had to do is send her a text." He took a drink of his water. "Next up is Owen Oldblood."

A few minutes later, a tall, handsome man in his mid-forties, dressed in a black suit with a teal tie, strolled across the cobblestone patio to our table. Alex and I both stood to shake his hand. When he grabbed hold of my hand, he lifted it to his lips and kissed the back. It left me speechless and a little creeped out.

"Lips to yourself, Vampire!" Needles flew off my shoulder, plucked a quill off his back, and stuck it on the tip of Owen's nose. *"You will treat the princess with respect. Or I'll cut out your tongue!"*

"It's okay, Needles," I said softly. "He didn't mean anything by it."

Alex growled. "I second whatever the porcupine said."

I glanced up in surprise at Alex's words. Or more the sound coming out of his throat. Harsh and low. That meant he was about to gargoyle out. Sure enough, his face was rock hard, and his eyes were glowing a deep red.

"Everyone settle down," I said. "Owen, you're gonna want to dial it down about one hundred percent."

"Of course." He dropped my hand, stepped back, and bowed. "I meant no disrespect."

"Don't make me cut out your lying tongue, Vampire!" Needles said, his wings a deep, angry red—the same color as Alex's eyes.

"I'm the only one who can understand you, Needles," I hissed. "And like I said, I got this handled."

"He talks?" Owen mused. "And you can understand him?"

"He does, and I can." I leveled Owen with a glare. "Now, if you'll sit, we can get started."

I glanced at Alex and was relieved to see he had himself back under control. I wasn't used to him getting jealous and territorial. I wasn't sure if I should be annoyed or flattered. But then I thought about what Needles had said about Gracie, and Alex not denying she was pretty and my response to that…I had no right to be annoyed at Alex's behavior. I'd responded the same way. I'd think about what all that meant later.

I rested my hands on the table. "You know about Nate Howler's death?"

"I do," Owen said.

"Just making sure," I said. "I knew from the way Gracie came out she'd been apprised of Nate's death. I just wasn't sure how to gauge your reaction."

Owen smiled. "Unlike Gracie, I just met Nate. Outside of our phone conversations, that is. I didn't have a personal connection with him. I'm saddened by his loss, of course. He'd have had quite the future in his field." Owen shrugged. "But, I guess it was not meant to be."

Alex shifted in his chair. "You are here on the island because your company is interested in acquiring the app Super Single? Is that right?"

"Correct."

"Walk us through the last two days you've been here," Alex said. "Starting with your arrival on Tuesday."

"Sure thing." Owen smoothed down his tie before speaking. "I arrived on the island around eleven. Checked into my room around eleven-fifty. Grabbed something to eat, then attended the two o'clock meeting in the conference room."

Alex looked down at his notes. "The meeting where Nate and Jordan pitched their app to the three buyers who came to acquire it?"

"Correct."

Alex nodded. "We understand there was some downtime after the two o'clock meeting. What did you do?"

Owen pursed his lips and looked up. "Let's see. I believe I changed into slacks and shirt, then strolled around the property for a while."

"Did you take out one of the magic carpets?" I asked.

Owen chuckled. "Guilty. I have to say, rather an ingenious idea. Magic carpets." His gaze shifted to me. "Then later that night, I received a text from Nate asking to meet for drinks in the bar. Typical during these types of acquisitions." He gave me a slow smile. "And everything was flowing along nicely, until Nate's girlfriend showed up. I believe her name is Anya. It was clear she was there to *stake* her claim on Nate." He chuckled. "A little vampire humor. But it was pathetic, really. I felt sorry for the poor girl. Hanging on Nate like a clinging vine. Made us all very uncomfortable—especially Gracie." He smirked. "A little funny, though."

"Why's that?" I asked.

"Anya is this buff, strong werewolf, and Gracie is this delicate and graceful pixie. And yet, Gracie seemed to come out on top with Nate. Not that it's good for Mavis or me. It didn't take the two of us long to recognize that Gracie had a history with Nate." He scowled. "Damn her company for playing up that angle."

"How did Nate react to Anya's obsessiveness?" I asked.

"He tried to ignore Anya, but it was hard to." One corner of his mouth lifted. "She can be rather…dramatic. When Nate left the table to answer a call on Tuesday night, Anya laid into Gracie." He put his hand over his chest. "Of course, I was about to step in and rescue poor Gracie, but she said she needed to use the restroom, and darn if that Anya didn't follow right after her."

"What did Nate and Mavis say?" I asked.

"Nate knew nothing about it because he'd left and was on the phone, of course. So when he came back in and only saw Mavis and me sitting at the table, I told him the other two girls went to the restroom." Owen smiled. "Mavis didn't say a word, just drank her martinis like they were going out of style. Something she's very good at."

"I take it Anya came back?" I asked.

"Oh, yes. Made some excuse about Gracie not feeling well, had too much to drink, and went to her room." He grinned so widely I could see his fangs. "I'm not sure any of us believed it, but no one was brave enough to call Anya a liar."

"And what about Wednesday?" Alex asked. "What did your day look like there?"

"I had breakfast in the restaurant. Afterward, I took a carpet out to the driving range and hit a few golf balls. I had a light lunch in my room and went over my presentation. I had the four o'clock slot to pitch my company and our ideas of where we saw the app going." He smiled. "The meeting went rather well, if I say so myself. Then, like the night before, I received a text from Nate asking to meet up again for drinks in the bar around nine."

"Did you go?" I asked.

"Oh, yes," he said. "It's like a train wreck. You want to look away, but can't. I figured Anya would be there again, and the girl drama would start." He shrugged. "And I was correct. Just small backbiting comments from Anya under her breath to Gracie. I'm not even sure if Nate caught them all. Then he went to the restroom, and the minute he was gone, Gracie grabbed her purse and ran out of the bar."

"Then what happened?" Alex asked.

"Anya picked up her purse and followed after Gracie."

I sat up straighter in my chair, and Needles dug his claws into my shoulder at my sudden movement. That declaration was news to Alex and me.

I leaned across the table. "You're saying Anya followed Gracie out of the bar Wednesday night?"

"Yes. By that time, I needed a refill. I think Mavis made a statement about seeing to them, but I can't remember. To be honest, I was bored with the whole jealous girlfriend thing and ready to retire to my room."

Alex looked up from his notepad, where he'd been jotting down notes about the fight. "Do you know of anyone who would have wanted to hurt Nate?"

Owen shrugged. "Well, with Nate out of the picture, I'm sure his partner, Jordan, will get control of the company. That's usually how that works, especially when the person isn't married." Again, he smiled wide enough for me to see his fangs. "Which actually may work out in my favor. I've only met him briefly, but from what I can tell, he's not the type of chap who will be controlled by his hormones—" He broke off and looked at me. "Excuse me. I meant to say, hopefully Jordan will make better choices than Nate seemed to be making regarding the company."

Sour grapes, as far as I was concerned. Owen was obviously jealous he didn't have the right body parts to sway Nate to go with his company. Which was a *huge* motive for Owen to take out Nate as far as I was concerned. He practically admitted to now having the upper hand in converting Jordan to his side.

"It also wouldn't surprise me if Mavis had a hand in Nate's death," Owen continued. "Did you know she was fired from her last firm? It was about six years ago, but she was let go because of unethical practices. Mavis thinks nothing of—well, let's just say *applying pressure* to her potential clients. Even a little stalking." He waved his hand dismissively in the air. "She's a big fish in the company she works for now, but she still makes half the income she used to at her old firm. Not good business practice, if you ask me, when your head closer resorts to mafia-style tactics to close a deal."

I thought about the phone conversation Gracie said she overheard where Mavis said it wouldn't be the first time she had to strong-arm a client to see her way.

Alex took a drink of his water. "I'm curious. What will happen if Jordan goes ahead with the selling of the app, and he goes with one of the other two women?"

Owen's smile faded. "What do you mean?"

"Well," Alex said, "one of the people we've interviewed already led us to believe if you didn't land this account, you'll probably be fired."

Red fiery rage flashed in Owen's eyes before he could clamp down on it. He didn't say anything for a few seconds, just ran his hands down his tie and breathed in deeply. "They're mistaken. I will admit that I've put a couple feelers out to other companies to see if anything better is available, but I'm happy where I am, and I don't plan on going anywhere."

Alex nodded, but I could tell he didn't believe Owen. "I'd like you to look at a note for me."

I picked up on my cue and slid the evidence bag containing the crumpled note toward Owen. "Do you recognize this?"

Owen read the note, and his eyebrows rose. "And the plot thickens. I don't know anything about the note, sorry."

"One last question," Alex said. "Can you tell us where you were last night from eleven to five this morning?"

Gone was any illusion of charm or casualness on Owen's part. He was now ramrod straight in his chair. "I was in my room. I retired around ten-thirty. Was asleep in my room by eleven. I didn't stir until around eight, when I came down to the restaurant for their breakfast buffet."

Alex nodded. "Thank you, Mr. Oldblood. That's all the questions we have right now."

Owen got up stiffly, nodded once to Alex, turned and bowed to me, then strode back inside the hotel.

Chapter Eleven

"You know what my favorite part about all this is?" I asked, once Owen left the table.

"What's that?"

"They all throw massive shade on the other suspects, but none on themselves."

Alex chuckled. "Did you expect anything different?"

"Nope. Just thought I'd make the observation."

"You know what I noticed?" Alex asked.

"What?"

"He never asked how Nate died." Alex drank from his glass. "So either he already knows how Nate died, or he doesn't give a darn how the young man died."

"Both are callous," I said.

I glanced at my watch and saw it was almost five-thirty. I'd been on the job with my game warden duties since eight, and then once I discovered Nate's body, we'd worked through lunch. I was starving, tired, and couldn't wait to change out of my uniform.

"Only one more interview," Alex said as he put his phone down. "I just texted Melody we were ready for Mavis Firestone." He winked at me. "Then you can run home and change out of your uniform."

I grinned at him. "You reading my mind, Gargoyle?"

He reached down and threaded his fingers through mine, giving them a light squeeze. "I just know you well enough by now."

"Speaking of knowing me by now," I said. "What was with the whole testosterone display? I mean, I expect it of Needles because he sees himself as my bodyguard, but I wasn't expecting that from you."

"Hey!" Needles stopped chewing on one of his salt sticks I'd given him out of my backpack. *"I am your bodyguard. That's my role."*

I waved him away and waited to hear what Alex had to say.

"I'm not sure," Alex said honestly. "I just didn't like the way he held your hand and kissed it. Like he had a right to." He grinned. "Made my gargoyle want to come out and play. And by play, I mean beat him to a bloody pulp."

I smiled. "As noble as that is, I can take care of myself."

"I'm aware, Witch. I've seen you in action plenty of times."

I raised my eyebrow at his playful tone. "Then remember those moments the next time your gargoyle comes to the surface. I can take care of myself."

He shrugged. "We'll see."

"Alex!"

But before I could continue, he gave my hand one last squeeze and stood to greet our last person of interest, Mavis Firestone.

Mavis was not what I expected. She towered over me, and I

was no wilting flower. I guessed her to be about six feet, with long flowing red hair, crystal blue eyes, and from the crow's feet around her eyes and mouth, maybe mid-fifties. Her black power suit was softened by the light blue camisole peeking out. I could feel her magic…and it was powerful, just like her.

"Ms. Firestone." Alex motioned to a chair across from us. "Please have a seat. I'm Sheriff Stone, and this is my partner, Agent Loci."

"You can call me Mavis," she offered.

"Mavis," Alex agreed as he looked down at his notes. "Your last name. Firestone? That makes you…"

Mavis smiled and crossed her legs. "An elemental witch."

"As you've been made aware," Alex continued, "Nate Howler is dead. And since he and his business partner, Jordan Owlman, are the reason you're here on the island, we'd like to ask you a few questions."

"Of course. I'm sorry to hear of his passing. I've tried to ask around how he died, but no one seems to know."

Alex nodded, but didn't answer her unspoken request. "We are aware of why you, Gracie Pixman, and Owen Oldblood are on the island. Can you walk us through the day you arrived?"

"I landed on Enchanted Island around eleven on Tuesday," Mavis said. "A car brought me out here to The Spellmoore. Such a magnificent place. This is my first time on Enchanted Island. My people are from Maine. I've always known of the island, of course, just never visited." She waved her hand through the air. "I tend to ramble. Anyway, I checked in, then attended the seminar Nate and Jordan gave at two." She gave me a sly smile. "I then met a nice young man in the bar who was also staying here. We had a couple drinks, which turned into a little dinner."

"And who is this man you met?" Alex asked.

Mavis tapped a long, red fingernail against her lips. "Let's see. I believe his name was Damon. He was just here for a couple days to relax. Left Wednesday morning. From Seattle, Washington area, I believe he said." She snapped her fingers. "Damon Nighthawk. Vampire."

"But he's no longer here?" Alex asked.

Mavis shook her head. "Sadly, no. But if you need to verify my story, perhaps one of the ladies behind the counter at the front desk can tell you when he checked in and out."

Alex nodded. "Did you bring Damon with you on Tuesday night when you met up with Nate and the others for drinks at the bar?"

Mavis laughed. "No, I did not. Damon was more of an after-dinner-drinks dessert, if you understand me? After our dinner, he retired to his room. He knew I still had business to conduct. I came down to the bar, had a couple drinks, then met back up with my young man around ten."

"Did anything unusual occur while having drinks at the bar with the others?" Alex asked.

Mavis' lips twisted into a wry smile. "You mean Nate's girlfriend storming in and making a scene? Entertainingly vile and typical of the youth today."

I smiled. I didn't want to like Mavis Firestone, but her no-nonsense attitude was one I appreciated. "What about Nate? How did he react?"

"He was embarrassed." She opened her clutch purse and withdrew a flat metal canister. "Do you mind if I smoke? Clove cigarettes."

"I thought those were illegal?" I said.

"Not if you make your own," Mavis said. "I love the smell. Very relaxing."

"I don't have a lighter," Alex said.

Mavis gave another of her throaty laughs, then conjured up a flame. "Fire elemental witch, remember?"

Mavis touched the tip of her homemade cigarette to the end of her flame, inhaled deeply, then blew out the smoke. I had to admit, it wasn't the worst smell.

Needles had a different reaction. He immediately sneezed, and his wings turned gray. *"I demand she put that fire sword out immediately!"*

We all stared open-mouthed as Needles dropped onto the tabletop, staggered back and forth, his wings pitch black...then suddenly keeled over like he'd died, his wings slowly closing over his body.

I smiled apologetically at Mavis. "I think that's Needles' way of asking you to please put out the clove cigarette."

Mavis nodded. "Of course. I didn't realize—what *is* that? A flying hedgehog?"

I groaned. Those were fighting words to Needles.

"He's a porcupine," I said quickly.

Needles unfolded his wings, opened one eye, and glared up at Mavis.

"I put it out, little porcupine," Mavis said. "I'm sorry."

Needles stood, huffed, and flew to my shoulder.

"I'm not sure where I was in my story," Mavis said.

"You witnessed the exchange between Anya and Gracie Tuesday night in the bar," I supplied.

"Right." Mavis shrugged. "That was really all it was. Nate got a phone call, and so he went outside to take it. Gracie went to the restroom, and Anya followed. Not sure what happened, but Anya came back and Gracie didn't. Anya gave some silly excuse about Gracie drinking too much, but we all knew it was a lie.

Thankfully, Nate came back, and the party broke up. I finished my drink then went to meet Damon."

"What about Wednesday?" Alex asked.

"Let's see. I had breakfast with Damon, then afterward he packed up and left. I had some time to kill, so I took a walk down to the large pond and watched the boaters for a while." She waggled her eyebrows at me. "Checked out the pickleball and tennis courts to ogle those men in shorts. And then I came back to the hotel and had a drink at the bar before heading back to my room."

"You didn't take out a magic carpet either day?" Alex asked.

"No. It was tempting, I admit. But I enjoy walking." She winked at Alex. "Keeps me in shape, Sheriff."

"Speaking of presentation," Alex said, ignoring her comment, "I take it you had the six o'clock time slot?"

"I did."

"Did you also meet up later that night again for drinks?" Alex asked.

"I did. And I'm sure you've heard all about the altercation that took place outside in a parking lot from Gracie herself. Poor thing."

"You'd be mistaken, smoking lady," Needles said.

"Actually," Alex said, "I'd like to take that part slowly."

"Sure. So I got to the bar around nine that night. It was later than normal because Nate and his girlfriend had a late dinner. After my presentation, Nate and Jordan both had questions. So I didn't leave until a little after seven. I grabbed a quick dinner myself, then went to the bar a little later."

"What happened when Nate left the table?" Alex asked.

Mavis smiled and shook her head. "He went to use the restroom, and Gracie tried to make her exit. She downed her drink, grabbed her purse, and hurried out of the bar. Anya did the same thing and followed after her."

"What did you and Owen do?" I asked.

Mavis sighed. "Owen said he was getting another drink, which left me to do the babysitting. I left out the same door they did, and I caught sight of Anya hurrying outside. It was dark out, but the lights around the building were on. I'll be honest, I figured she'd turn right. Like maybe Gracie wanted to take a walk by the pond or something like that, but Anya took a left. I walked out, took a left, took another left at the end of the building, then followed at a safe distance." She shrugged. "I'm not sure what I thought I could do, but I trailed behind."

"What happened?" I asked.

"Toward the middle of the building, Anya caught up with Gracie. They were in a side parking lot area, so there was overhead lighting. Enough I could see, anyway. The two started arguing, then Anya reached out and hit Gracie in her face. Gracie screamed and grabbed for Anya's hair. The two girls went down and started rolling around on the ground. I ran to separate them, and that's when someone who works here stepped out of her car and helped me separate the two women."

Alex frowned. "Do you know who the other woman was who helped you?"

Mavis shook her head. "Never saw her before. She was dressed like our server, so possibly she worked in the restaurant or bar area."

"*Funny how both Gracie and Anya left this entire story out,*" Needles said.

I nodded in agreement.

"*Wanna bet the parking lot Smoking Lady is talking about also leads to the kitchen?*" Needles said. "*The same kitchen where the murder weapon was stolen from?*"

Again I nodded.

"What happened next?" Alex asked.

"Nothing. The two girls separated, hissing and spitting insults. I had ahold of Gracie. I told her to take a walk and cool off. She headed toward the back of the hotel. I have no idea where she went exactly. The other girl let Anya go, and I told Anya if she knew what was good for her, she'd run back inside to her boyfriend." Mavis grinned. "I may have had both palms on fire when I said it. Who knows? I can't remember." She chuckled. "She hurried back inside like her tail was on fire."

"What did you do after that?" I asked.

Mavis shrugged. "I waited until the other woman got back safely in her car and left. I then went around to the back of the hotel and sat on the patio overlooking the small pond they have back there. They have these pretty little lights that change color all around the pond and even have some that float in the pond. It was very relaxing. I probably sat out there until eleven or a little after. Then I went inside and went to my room."

"Did you ever see Gracie return?" Alex asked.

Mavis shook her head. "No."

"So you were in your room," Alex said, "from eleven until when the next morning?"

Mavis shrugged. "I'd say around breakfast. I rang for a coffee, croissant, and fresh fruit from room service."

Alex pointed to my note, and I slid it over to her.

"Do you recognize this note?" I asked.

Mavis read over it then handed it back to me. "No. But I do recognize the stationery. I believe I have some in my room. Plus, I've seen it all around the hotel."

Alex nodded. "Do you know of anyone who might want to hurt Nate?"

"Other than the girlfriend?" Mavis mused. "Not really. But

I'll drop some gossip, since I'm sure my other two competitors have gossiped about me to you." She settled back in her chair. "On Wednesday, right before I went in for my private pitch to Nate and Jordan, I saw Owen and Nate in a heated exchange in the hallway. I couldn't hear what was said, I was too far away." She gave me a smile. "And before I could perform an amplification spell, the exchange was done."

"What exactly is an amplification spell?" Alex asked. "A spell that allows you to eavesdrop on other people's conversations?"

"Something like that," Mavis said.

Alex sent me a stare, and I knew he was wondering if I'd ever done that to him. I rolled my eyes and focused on Mavis.

"And Gracie?" I asked.

Mavis shrugged. "I don't know any gossip about her, except that she's the girl to beat because she and Nate have history."

"What if I told you someone overheard you on the phone Tuesday?" Alex mused. "They heard you say something like it wouldn't be the first time you'd gotten your hands dirty when it came to a client?"

Mavis snorted. "That must have come from Gracie, since she's right across the hall from me." She leaned forward and smiled. "Witch, remember? I was aware she was there, Sheriff. I said that just to get a rise out of her. A power play on my part, if you will." She shrugged. "My way of intimidating the competition." She smiled and leaned back in her chair. "I see it worked. You see, I did a background check via the internet and social media to get a little dirt on Gracie Pixman and Owen Oldblood. I wanted to know what would push their buttons. Gracie is the youngest and newest in this business, so I didn't really see her as a threat...until I learned she was from Enchanted Island *and* she'd dated Nate at one time. That's when I knew she'd be my biggest competition when it came down to it." She sighed. "Because the heart will always win in the end."

"You realize that makes you a prime suspect?" Alex asked.

Mavis laughed. "Sheriff, if I wanted to eliminate the competition, I'd have killed Gracie, not the leading man of the company I want to snag. I'm not even sure right now where we stand on the deal."

Chapter Twelve

"Thanks for driving me to get my Bronco." I shut Alex's door and opened my driver's side door for Needles to fly in. "I really appreciate it. Don't forget to drop off the crumpled note tonight so Finn can get to it tomorrow."

"I won't." He turned me around and drew me close. "I guess this is goodbye. Seeing as how you're spending the night with Serena at The Spellmoore."

I grinned and wound my arms around his neck. "I guess it is."

He lowered his mouth to mine, and I lost myself in the feel of his lips and his body pressed against me. I'm not sure how long we stood there lost in our kiss…but I soon became aware of a thumping sound behind me. Breaking off the kiss, I turned and saw Needles' face plastered against the back window, his little paw pounding on the glass.

I sighed. "I guess this means good night."

Alex grinned and kissed me quickly again. "I guess so."

His cell phone beeped, and he withdrew it from his pocket.

"Doc says knife to the heart is what killed Nate. No other mortal wounds or blows. Time of death harder to pinpoint since he was submerged in water. Guess is between eleven to one in the morning."

"Not that it matters," I said. "Supposedly, everyone was in bed asleep."

Alex chuckled. "Yeah. We're gonna need to break those alibis." He kissed me again. "Text me when you and Serena get to The Spellmoore and head to bed?"

"Of course."

"Meet up at the bakery tomorrow around eight?" Alex asked.

"Sounds good."

I stashed my suitcase in the back of the Bronco and motioned for Needles. "Let's go. I want to talk with dad, but I also need to be back at The Spellmoore within the hour."

"I'm ready." Needles perched on the open window ledge. *"You packed my toothbrush, pajamas, and cotton balls, right? You have a tendency to snore."*

I rolled my eyes. "I don't snore. And, yes, I packed your stuff."

"Then let's go see Black Forest King. I spoke with him a little today through our link to communicate, but I didn't want to say too much."

"I appreciate it."

I rolled my shoulders, did a couple stretches, then took off jogging around the back of the castle—the home Dad had built for Mom when he found out she was pregnant with me.

For a few minutes, it was only Needles and me on the path. I could hear his buzzing wings beside me in the still summer night, and it brought me comfort. After a few more minutes of quiet jogging, an enormous ball of light zipped my way and broke into giggling pieces when it neared us. The lightning bugs had come to play and light my way.

"*We hear something happened today, Princess!*"

"*Black Forest King said you were on the north side of the island. How exciting!*"

"*Did you see the gargoyle today?*"

"*He's so handsome!*"

"*Black Forest King is worried about you.*"

"*Did you bring us any treats?*"

On and on they went as Needles and I neared the entrance of Black Forest. Usually Needles was more talkative and joked with the lightning bugs, but tonight he was strangely silent. He was obviously worried about what my dad was going to say about the murder, seeing as it was so close to the north side of the island.

I came to a stop in front of my favorite pine tree and waited until he lifted his branch off the forest floor. "*Lovely to see you, Princess. Welcome home.*"

"Thank you."

For me, the first initial impact of Black Forest was pure euphoria—peaceful and serene. The minute I stepped inside Dad's domain…everything was right in the world.

Dad was a genius loci. That meant he was the heart and soul of Black Forest. And it showed. Everywhere I looked, every breath I inhaled…I could feel his presence and essence.

It was like having thousands of years of wonderful memories and emotions flooding your body.

"*I love coming home,*" Needles said. "*I always feel better.*"

"Me too."

We raced through the dense forest. It didn't take long for the trees to fall away and for us to enter the vast green clearing where Dad lived.

My Dad. The most magnificent tree I'd ever seen.

I paused to catch my breath and take him in. His tree roots were at least four feet tall and extended out of the ground about twenty feet from the base of the tree. His trunk was one hundred twenty feet around, and his branches—which averaged about thirty to forty feet—were strong and thick.

"Shayla." Dad's voice rumbled in my head. *"Daughter of my Heart. How are you? I've missed you."*

Hearing his words, I jumped up onto one of his roots, ran down the length of him, then plopped down at his base, closed my eyes, and leaned back against his trunk. "Hey, Dad. I've missed you too."

I felt a leaf brush my cheek and smiled. Being in Dad's presence always made me feel cherished. I'd learned recently, when I'd been shot, that I could heal faster than most supernaturals—even werewolves. Dad said there was a reason he was thousands of years old and in great health. But when I pressed him for more information, he said he'd tell me when the time was right.

I'd inherited a lot from Black Forest King. According to him, the ability to speak to the animals and forest and plants and to heal quickly was just the tip of the iceberg. I figured I could wait for the rest of the surprise.

"I hear you had a rough day," Dad said. *"Can you tell me about it?"*

And so I sat there, knees drawn to my chin, and told him everything from the moment I reached the magnificent waterfall and geyser to the time Alex dropped me off at my Bronco.

"I warned you the north side of the forest could be dangerous," Dad said.

"I know, Dad. But this had nothing to do with the forest itself, and everything to do with an evil supernatural."

"You are right, Shayla. I just don't want to admit the island is changing."

"We'll figure this out," I said. "Alex and I are starting back first thing in the morning."

"You will discover the killer. Of this, I have no doubt." Dad was silent a minute. *"I think it is a wonderful idea to have Serena's wedding at The Spellmoore."*

"You know about The Spellmoore?"

Dad's laughter filled my head. *"Of course. When Sebastian Spellmoore sent word through one of the original witch families that he'd like to build a resort on the island, I had to give my approval because of the location. I knew it was close to the border, but I went ahead and said yes. He assured me through the witches that he had provisions set in place to keep other supernaturals away."*

"The large rocks. They definitely are a deterrent," I agreed. "It'll be a beautiful place for Serena to get married."

Dad chuckled. *"Maybe Serena won't be the only one to get married there?"*

Needles zipped over to me and laughed. *"If the kissing I saw tonight keeps up, you might need to put some pressure on the gargoyle, Black Forest King."*

"Shut up, Needles." I swatted playfully at him. "No one is asking you."

"As much as I love having you here, Daughter, I don't want to keep you. You must go and solve your crime. Nate Howler and his parents deserve to know what happened to him."

"I know." I stood and hugged his trunk. "I love you, Dad."

"And I you, Shayla." He paused. *"Take care of my forest and animals."*

"I will. I promise."

"*And, Needles, take care of my heart. She means the world to me. The island can be a dangerous place.*"

Needles, his wings a deep purple, gave Dad a salute. "*With my life, Black Forest King.*"

I said goodnight to dad, and Needles and I headed out of Black Forest and back down the path that led to the Bronco in my driveway. Once inside, I handed Needles a salt stick, buckled him in, and headed for The Spellmoore and Serena.

Chapter Thirteen

"It's absolutely gorgeous," my cousin, Serena, said as she stepped inside our room. "I had no idea The Spellmoore was this amazing."

"Me, neither."

"I mean, if this is just the cheapest room they have," she continued, "can you imagine what one of the suites on the second and third floor must look like?"

I rolled my suitcase past a fully stocked hidden bar on my left, a pocketed door I figured led to the bathroom a little farther down on the right, and then stopped to take in the rest of the expensively decorated room. It was done in mostly baby blue, gray, cream, and white, with two double beds taking up a large portion of one wall, an ornate cream armoire that had been distressed and converted into a TV stand and dresser directly across from the beds, a paisley wingback chair and ottoman to the right of the armoire, and a small desk pushed against the half wall to the left of the armoire. Everything about the room screamed luxury—from the bedding to the tear-drop crystal chandelier.

"I've seen the rooms on the second floor," I said. "And while they have a kitchenette and extended bedroom, trust me, this room is just as nicely furnished."

"I'm going to sleep," Needles said as he settled down on the chair. *"Don't keep me up all night with your giggling and girl stuff."*

I was about to growl at him, when he wrapped his wings over his body and immediately fell into a deep sleep. Tiny snores soon followed.

"I'm glad I wasted time packing your crap," I hissed.

"Oh, my goodness," Serena whispered. "Look at this bathroom."

I strolled over to where she stood and peeked inside. The gray and white tile showcased a shower to die for…multi-jets on each side of the wall with a waterfall showerhead on the ceiling. An L-shaped gray and white marble counter held a sink on each side, complete with silver and glass accessories. It was also the size of my master bathroom in the castle.

I heard a squeal and turned to see Serena holding up a long white fluffy robe. "We each have our own robe!"

I laughed. "It's summer, you nut. You can't wear that."

"Watch me."

I headed out of the bathroom, down the short hallway, to the fully stocked bar. I was more interested in what *that* held than fluffy robes that would probably suffocate me.

"This is all complimentary?" I demanded. "You're sure?"

"That's what the concierge said." Serena laughed. "Who knew there was a place fancier than your castle on Enchanted Island? Oh, and did you see that massive body of water as you drove down the driveway? The sun was going down, so I didn't get a great view, but I think they have boats you can rent."

"They do." I grabbed two wine glasses, a bottle of cabernet, and the wine opener. "Let's have a drink."

Serena sat in the middle of her bed, the white robe wrapped snuggly around her. She grinned at me when I walked in and saw her. "Told ya I was gonna wear it." She waved a paper menu at me. "It says they serve dinner until nine. You hungry?"

"I ate a sandwich while I packed." I set the glasses down and opened and poured the wine. "I just wish Tamara was here with us. But I know how that honeymoon period is at first in a relationship."

Serena took a glass from me and grinned. "Yeah. She's really happy. And she enjoys going over to Zach's place early to spend time with the baby before he gets home at night after his bartending shift."

I smiled, pleased as punch that I'd helped to bring those two together. "So, do we talk wedding or murder first?"

Serena laughed. "Since I'm going to get a tour of this place tomorrow after the bakery closes, how about we talk murder?" Serena took a sip of her wine. "But I can already tell this will definitely be the venue for my wedding."

We toasted The Spellmoore and the upcoming wedding. "Now you just need to set a date."

Serena laughed. "I think we're about to settle on that. But finding a place was most important." She covered her leg with the robe. "Now, dish on what you discovered today."

Since Serena was often deputized when we were shorthanded on the island, it was okay for me to talk about the case with her. I brought her up-to-date on the suspects and their interviews.

"Motive for Jordan?" Serena asked.

"By killing Nate, he now has one hundred percent control of the company."

"But he doesn't like the limelight," Serena pointed out. "He doesn't even go to the bar for drinks with everyone."

"Right, but he'll get all three hundred thousand dollars."

Serena nodded. "Yeah, that's a pretty powerful motive. But he also killed his best friend and business partner to get it." She smiled. "And the crazy girlfriend?"

I laughed. "Anya Moony. She's like a walking cliché, but that doesn't mean I'm willing to discount her. Jealousy and anger are *strong* motives to kill. Right up there with money and greed."

"Going back to Jordan," Serena said.

I nodded. "Exactly. But the other three suspects aren't innocent either. Although, I will admit I'm not exactly sure what motive Gracie Pixman has to kill Nate. I can't think of a single thing she would gain by killing him."

"Maybe she's lying, and the meetings weren't going as well as she claims," Serena said. "Maybe she knew Nate and Jordan would go with one of the others. After all, they have more experience than she does. Maybe that was enough to make her snap. Her company sent her because they knew she had a relationship with Nate, and they were banking on that past relationship landing them this huge account. Maybe she thought by killing Nate, she could somehow appeal to Jordan to go with her company during this difficult time. Like they were bonding."

I shook my head in amazement. "Wow. That's actually a great motive. I was thinking small and personal, not broad like you. That's actually good."

Serena smirked and took a drink of her wine. "I have my moments."

I laughed. "Then we have Owen Oldblood. He tries to play the charming "good ol' boys" guy, says just the right things. But I don't like him. We were told if he didn't land this account, then he'd be fired from his company. He admitted he was looking, but it didn't have anything to do with his company firing him if he didn't land this account. Didn't ring true at all. I think he was lying."

"And Mavis Firestone?"

I drained the last of my wine and smiled. "I like her. She's like this witchy cougar lady." I poured us both more wine. "She unapologetically admitted to picking up this much younger guy in the bar and staying the night with him her first night here!"

Serena gasped. "And it was true?"

"Yes. After Alex dropped me off at my vehicle tonight, he went back to The Spellmoore to talk with Melody. Alex didn't tell her why he wanted this guy's name, but Melody told him she remembered who the guy was because he'd tried to buy *her* a drink one night at the bar, but she declined because she thought he was too young for her!"

Serena laughed. "Scandalous!"

"But anyway, back to Mavis and her motive. She's the oldest of the three. Owen said she was fired from her last job because of unethical practices. Gracie said she overheard Mavis on the phone saying she had no problem strongarming Nate because she'd done it before. Of course, Mavis claims she knew Gracie was there and was just trying to intimidate her, but I don't doubt for one minute Mavis would be capable of applying pressure to a client."

"But how would killing Nate give the other two—Owen and Mavis—the edge?"

"That's easier for me to see," I said. "Gracie is distraught. She's seriously upset. I don't think her head is in this anymore. Both Mavis and Owen admitted they knew about Gracie's previous relationship with Nate, plus both witnessed Anya going after Gracie for two nights in a row. They knew Gracie was fragile. By killing off Nate, Gracie is pretty much out of the equation, leaving just two candidates on the table. And let's face it, Jordan Owlman doesn't have the chops for business or entertaining clients like Nate had. He'd be easy to convert."

"And all of them have the same alibi for Wednesday night?" Serena mused. "Alone in their rooms from eleven on?"

"Yep." I grinned. "Someone's a liar."

Serena downed the last of her wine and set the empty glass on the bedside table we shared. "I need to go to bed. I have to be at the bakery by four-thirty."

"I told Alex to meet me at your shop at eight. We need to do some more digging. We need to talk to Doc and Finn, and then I want to question the staff here again."

Serena unbelted her robe and slid under her covers. "You know you might get more juicy info if you wait for me to question staff and suspects tomorrow night."

I set my empty glass next to hers and nodded. "I'd already thought of that. I figured Friday night, you and me down at the bar."

"I like it!" she said. "Grant and Alex may not, but if we remind them we're taking on this sacrifice in order to find a killer, they might understand."

I laughed and shut off the light. "Did I mention tomorrow night was karaoke night?"

"Hot damn."

Chapter Fourteen

I wasn't the least bit surprised to see Alex already at Enchanted Bakery & Brew the next morning. Usually I beat him to Serena's and Tamara's shop, but this morning I'd been dragging. I was going to need double the caffeine just to function.

"Maybe next time you won't stay up drinking and laughing half the night," Needles snickered as I opened the bakery's front door.

"We were in bed by ten, *Porcupine*," I sneered.

I held the door open wider so two customers could file out.

Needles did his wheezy, high-pitch laugh in my ear. *"Guess this means you're getting too old to do this kind of stuff. For you, Princess, forty* isn't *the new twenty."*

"Shut up," I growled. "Or no extra salty sticks for you."

Needles flew off my shoulder, did a somersault in the air, and laughed some more.

"Hey, Needles," Zoie said from behind the counter. "Are you picking on Shayla?"

"Maybe just a little."

"What's new with you, Miss Zoie?" I asked, sidling up next to Alex.

A blush spread across her cheeks. "Not much. I have my first date tonight with Brick."

Alex growled softly, and I swatted him playfully on the arm. "How're you feeling about that?"

"Okay." Zoie laughed. "I'm lying. I'm totally nervous."

"What're you guys doing?" I pointed to a cranberry muffin in the display case. "Dinner or something else?"

Zoie dropped my muffin in a white bag. "We're doing the family movie in the park thing. So I'm making us up a picnic basket of food, and he's bringing the blanket."

"That sounds like a lot of fun," I said. "What's playing?"

"*Casper*," Zoie said.

I frowned. "Like the ghost?"

"Exactly." Zoie set the bag on the counter next to my extra-large coffee. "It's an oldie move. From like the nineteen nineties, I think?"

"Brat." I flicked my wrist and sent her sliding backward across the floor. "The nineties are not old."

Laughing, Zoie grabbed hold of the display case to keep herself grounded. "My apologies. I didn't mean old, I meant *antique*."

"Not helping yourself, Zoie," Serena said dryly as she rang up my order.

I snatched up my muffin and coffee and gave Zoie a mock glare. "You better behave yourself tonight."

She grinned. "I'm always well behaved."

Alex grunted.

"What time is he picking you up?" I asked.

"Around six. Movie starts at seven."

"I'll text you good luck," I promised.

When Alex turned to walk toward the door, I turned back to Zoie. "And let me know if he kisses you goodnight."

"I heard that!" Alex yelled.

* * *

Doc Drago's laboratory was in the basement of the sheriff's office—as were the IT and forensics labs. And manning the ship with a tight fist was Pearl Earthly, an eighty-year-old dragon lady. Technically, she was a witch, but she guarded her lair like a dragon guards treasure. No one got in or out unless she said so. Her twin sister, Opal Earthly, ran the sheriff's station upstairs with the same iron fist.

Needles stayed in the Blazer since dead bodies weren't really his thing. Alex rolled down the windows, and I tossed him a salty stick to chew on.

Sure enough, Pearl was sitting behind her desk knitting when Alex and I walked down the stairs.

"How's it going, Pearl?" I asked.

"Can't complain." She set her knitting down and frowned. "I don't have you on the books."

Alex crossed his arms over his chest. "I'm sure you know Doc has a body back there."

"Perhaps," Pearl said. "But it really wouldn't kill you to make an appointment ahead of time, Sheriff. It's always been done that way. Our old sheriff knew the rules."

"How are the Caraway Twins?" I asked, hoping to steer the conversation away from the age-old argument the two of them always had. It also gave Alex enough time to text Doc and let him know we were there.

An honest-to-goodness blush crept over Pearl's wrinkled,

thin skin. "They're doing just fine. Thank you for asking, Shayla."

I'd found out a couple weeks ago that Pearl and Opal were dating Herb and Basil Caraway, twin brothers who also happened to be kitchen witches. They'd moved to the island three months ago when their one-hundred-year-old mother passed away. They decided to keep her house and stay on the island. The men were actually younger than the spinster twin sisters, which had the town buzzing.

"I suppose I can see if Doc wants to speak with you," Pearl said, giving Alex the evil eye.

Before she could pick up the phone, Doc hollered from down the hall to send us back. Pearl narrowed her eyes at Alex. "One day, young man, I'll figure out how you do that."

I smothered the laugh that wanted to come out.

Doc met us at his door. "I really don't have anything more for you, but I believe Finn has the tox report back."

"Thanks, Doc."

Alex slapped Doc Drago on the shoulder, and we continued down the hall until we came to the last door on the right. I knocked, and Finn hollered for us to enter.

Finnigan "Finn" Faeton was a five-foot-nothing fairy with multi-colored spiked hair, body tattoos, and piercings in her nose, eyebrows, and ears. She was the exact opposite of what you'd think a forensics technician would look like. But I knew first-hand she was the best in her field. My old employer, the government, tried countless times to get her to work for them.

"What up, peeps?" Finn asked as she looked up from her paperwork.

Alex smiled. "Just coming to see what you have on Nate Howler."

"He was clean," Finn said. "No illegal or prescription drugs found in blood or urine. There was alcohol, but other than that, I really have nothing that would make me think deeper testing is needed. No unknown substances, nothing suspicious."

"That helps," Alex said.

"Now," Finn continued, "as far as the samples go. The scrape from the magic carpet was blood, and it was a positive match to Nate Howler. However, no fingerprints or traces of DNA could be found on the stationery note."

Alex nodded. "So we know Nate was bleeding on the magic carpet before he ended up in the river."

"Which makes our supposition possible," I said. "He was stabbed in the woods, lifted onto the magic carpet, then tossed over into the river."

"I hear the murder happened out at The Spellmoore," Finn said. "Fancy place. My little cousin, Petra, works out there. She's a server in the restaurant and bar. Says the tips are amazing."

"I'll look for her tonight," I said. "Serena and I are hitting the bar, but I'm sure we'll do dinner first."

"Is that so?" Alex mused. "You're hitting the bar?"

Finn laughed. "Righteous. Can I go too? Maybe you need a quirky, free-spirited fairy to ease the way for you?"

I laughed. "Sure. What time do you get off?"

"Around five."

"Let's say dinner around six," I said. "We have a room there, so you can crash with us."

"Awesome. I'll see ya there."

We stepped back out into the hallway. Before we could continue, the door across the hall opened, and IT specialist Gordon Hoots greeted us.

"I know you probably can't tell me anything," he said, "seeing as how my nephew is Jordan Owlman, but I know my nephew. He's a brilliant kid, but not worldly or savvy. Nate was more than his best friend, he was like his idol." He looked away and cleared his throat. "I tried to get Jordan to put a stop to the rest of the meetings out there. Those three companies will understand he needs some time, but he's so distraught. He's not thinking right. He says he just wants to wash his hands of this." He sighed. "I'm afraid that may mean one or more of them may try and take advantage of Jordan during this time." He shrugged and looked at us sheepishly. "I thought maybe that might go to motive for any of those three buyers too."

Alex nodded. "I understand your worry, Gordon. Thanks for the heads up."

Gordon nodded, stepped back inside his office, and closed his door. We didn't say anything until we were back in Alex's Blazer.

"So?" Alex mused. "What do you think about Gordon's theory that one of the three others may try and strike quickly to get Jordan to sell?"

"I've actually thought the same thing."

"Me too." Alex pulled out onto the street. "But I keep circling back to who would gain the most from Nate's death, and it's hands-down Jordan."

"I agree with the Gargoyle," Needles said. *"As much as I hate to say it."*

Alex's cell phone dinged with an incoming text. Alex tossed me his phone, and I pulled up the text and read it aloud. "It's Grant. He says he's hoping to have all the background on the five suspects by the afternoon, but he needs to take an hour personal time around four."

"Text him we'll stop by the station around three then."

"Why drive back in?" I asked. "I know where he's going. He and Serena are touring The Spellmoore to decide whether or not to have their wedding there. I'll just have him bring the background reports with him. Two birds, one stone, and all that."

I texted Grant and told him to bring the reports with him when he went to The Spellmoore, and then I texted Serena and told her to invite Tamara to our girls' night out. A few minutes later, Serena texted back Zach had the night off, so he and Tamara were taking Baby Jaden to the local pool and then grabbing dinner out afterward.

"So where to now?" I asked.

"Let's go take another look at the original crime scene. See if anything jumps out."

Chapter Fifteen

"Do you really think we overlooked something?" I asked as Alex and I ambled down the cement walkway behind the hotel.

"Probably not," Alex said, "but sometimes going back to the scene of the crime later helps to look at things a different way. Plus, now that we know for sure it was Nate's blood on the carpet, maybe we'll see something different."

"He's reaching," Needles said as he fluttered his iridescent wings near my face.

I grinned at him to let him know I agreed.

"I can hear you two," Alex said dryly.

"What?" I laughingly protested.

"You think I'm grasping at straws," he said.

"Never," I deadpanned.

We reached the end of the sidewalk. Straight ahead was nothing but big boulders and rocks. The sidewalk curved left to take visitors to the magic carpets or farther down to the golf range if they wanted to go by foot. We took a right into the thicket of dense trees and shrubs.

The crime scene tape was still up, which I took as a good sign. We hadn't advertised where Nate had been killed, but gossip even among the staff could spread quickly.

"You take that area over there," Alex said, pointing to my left. "And I'll look over here."

"And I'll go talk to the animals again. See if they've seen anything more."

I squatted down and waved my hands over a section of grass. I didn't want to touch anything just in case, so I used my magic to part the tall grass and look around. I did this inch by agonizing inch…but in the end, I still didn't find anything relevant.

"Got anything?" I called out.

"Nothing." Alex sidled up next to me. "I knew it was a long shot, but I—"

He was cut off when Needles came charging out of the woods, his crimson wings beating so fast they sounded like a gnat buzzing around my ear. He came to an abrupt stop inches from us.

"I got something," he panted. *"I talked with Gabe, the rabbit from the other day who ran with us, and he said he heard that Skip, a reclusive squirrel, found something but won't tell anyone."*

"What's he saying?" Alex asked.

"He said Gabe, the rabbit who helped us the other day, heard through the grapevine that Skip the Squirrel may have something we need."

Alex blinked a couple times. "You're kidding? That is both so cool and so weird."

I laughed, then turned to Needles. "Where is Skip?"

"Hiding. He's too scared to come out of his tree."

"We need to go see Skip," I said to Alex. "He's too scared to come to us."

Alex bowed. "Lead the way, Princess."

I narrowed my eyes at him. "Watch it."

But Alex just grinned.

We followed Needles farther into the woods, heading toward the river. The closer we got to the water, the closer together the trees became. For Needles, it was easy to zip in and out of the branches and small clearings, but for Alex and me, it was tougher to traverse.

"Here." Needles stopped at a large oak, hovering near the trunk. *"Skip has the first hole about six feet up."*

"Will he come down?" I asked.

Needles shook his head. *"He's too scared."*

"Give me a minute," I said to Alex. "Skip is too scared to come out of his house. I think he's afraid he's going to get in trouble."

Alex grinned. "Go do your thing."

"You stay here too," I said to Needles. "You have a tendency to scare the wild animals outside Black Forest."

I closed my eyes, whispered the levitation spell, and slowly ascended into the air. When I reached the hole Needles told me about, I peeked inside.

"Hello? Skip, are you in there?"

I could hear chirping inside, then a few seconds later, a wide-eyed squirrel popped out. *"Princess? Is that really you? You came to my home?"*

"I did," I said. "And a lovely home it is."

He lifted his front paws and started wringing them. *"Please don't be mad at me, Princess. I didn't mean to take it. It's just it was so shiny and pretty. I had to have it."*

I held up a hand. "I'm not angry, Skip. In fact, I have no idea what it is you even found."

He drew back his lips and chattered his teeth. At this rate, the poor squirrel was going to give himself a heart attack. I reached out and ran my hand over his head, whispering words of comfort.

"Do you want it back?" Skip asked once he'd composed himself.

"I'd like to see it first," I said. "Maybe I won't need it."

Fat chance, since I had the feeling Skip found something at the crime scene. A few seconds later, Skip returned, his paws clasped tightly together. Like the butterfly from yesterday, I could feel his anxiety rolling off him in waves. He wanted to show me, but he also didn't want to lose his treasure.

"May I see?" I asked gently.

Skip nodded and slowly opened his paws.

A diamond earring stud twinkled up at me.

"It's beautiful," I said.

"But mine? Right?"

"Skip, you know a man was badly hurt out here, right?"

The squirrel closed his paws over the diamond earring and nodded.

"What you have in your paw could help us prove who hurt him."

"Oh."

"Can I ask you where you found your beautiful treasure?"

"By the ribbon."

"The ribbon?" I frowned, trying to understand what he was saying. "Oh, you mean the crime scene tape? Okay. So you found it near the ribbon?"

He nodded his head emphatically. "By the ribbon."

"I'll tell you what?" I said. "How about we trade?"

His ears perked up. *"Trade? What do you mean?"*

I reached inside the front pocket of my uniform and withdrew the black tourmaline crystal Black Forest King had given me on my first day as the game warden on Enchanted Island. It had protected me against several close calls since taking the job.

I showed Skip the small crystal. "Black Forest King gave this to me. How about I give it to you, and you give me what you have?"

Skip's eyes were huge. *"Black Forest King!"* The awe in his voice made me smile. I knew he could feel the magic rolling off the crystal, and there was no way he could turn it down. He slowly reached out one paw and touched the stone. *"Oh! Magic."*

"Yes. I'll trade you the crystal for your earring."

"Deal!"

He shoved the earring at me and snatched the black tourmaline out of my hand. He held it against his face, and this time when his teeth chattered, I got the impression it was a good thing.

"Thank you, Skip, for the trade."

"Thank you, Princess. I will cherish this always."

I'd planned on levitating both me and the earring down so I didn't have to touch it, but since Skip shoved it in my hand, that was now out of the question. Not that it probably mattered. He'd had his paws all over it, and goodness only knew where it had been stored inside his home in the tree trunk. With one last wave to Skip, I slowly lowered myself to where Alex and Needles waited.

"Well?" Alex said.

"Did you give that petty thief the tourmaline crystal Black Forest King gave you?" Needles demanded.

"How about the two of you give me a second," I said. "Geez. Yes, Needles, I gave my protection crystal to Skip. I'm sure Dad will give me another one. And as for what he gave me..." I held out my hand and showed Alex the diamond earring. "I didn't want to touch it, but now it doesn't matter. Perhaps we can still get something off it."

"Did Skip tell you where he found the earring?" Alex asked.

"By the ribbon," I said. "Which I took to mean the crime scene tape."

Alex nodded. "So maybe the killer dropped it? Or somehow it was ripped out if there was a struggle or scuffle?"

"However it came to be there," I said, "I think we can narrow our suspects down to Anya, Gracie, or Mavis."

"True," Alex said. "I can't see Jordan or Owen wearing an earring."

I snorted. "I'd love to see Owen wearing it."

Alex gave me a side eye.

"The gargoyle is jealous," Needles said, his wings shimmering green. *"That's funny. Is he worried he's gonna be replaced by a hand-kissing vampire?"*

"Hush," I said.

"He's talking about me again, isn't he?" Alex mused.

I grinned. "Of course."

"Let's head back to the hotel and see if anyone has reported a missing or lost earring," Alex said. "Could be they didn't realize they lost it down here."

Ten minutes later, Alex and I entered the front doors of The Spellmoore...Needles hitching a ride on my shoulder. A young woman was behind the front desk, talking to Melody.

"Hello," Melody said. "Is everything okay? Or do you need to speak with me?"

"I was wondering," Alex said, "has anyone—guest or staff member—reported a missing earring?"

Melody's eyes widened before she excused herself and

motioned for us to follow her into her office. She shut the door and moved toward her desk. "I'm trying to keep the staff out of the loop. Less gossip that way."

"I understand," Alex said.

Melody sat behind her desk and motioned for us to have a seat as well. "I have had a guest report a missing diamond earring. I believe she reported it missing Thursday morning. She said she went to put it on, and it wasn't on her nightstand like it was supposed to be. She was very upset. Threatened to call the police if it wasn't returned to her immediately. She was sure one of the cleaning ladies palmed it. I assured her that would never happen." Melody sighed. "I have to admit, when you first showed up yesterday, I thought maybe she *had* called you guys. I'm still searching everywhere for it. I guess she must have told you about it if you're asking after it?"

"Something like that," Alex said. "Can you tell me who the guest was that reported the earring missing?"

"Of course. Gracie Pixman."

Chapter Sixteen

"What is this about?" Gracie asked as she hurried off the elevator and over to where we stood by the indoor fountain. "Did you find out who killed Nate?"

"Sure did," Needles said from his perch on my shoulder. *"And we're looking at you, Sister."*

"No," Alex said. "Not yet. This is about your diamond earring you reported stolen."

That brought her up short. "Oh. What about it?"

I'd gotten an evidence bag out of Alex's Blazer before we went in to question Melody about the earring. I held up the bagged earring inches from her face. "Is this it?"

"Yes."

She went to reach for the bag, but I pulled it back. "I'm afraid it's in an evidence bag for a reason. Where did you say you last saw this earring?"

"On my bedside table," Gracie said.

"You're sure?" I pressed.

"Yes."

"That's odd," I continued, "because we just discovered this earring near the crime scene tape where Nate was killed."

Gracie gasped and staggered backward. "What? That's impossible."

It actually *was* a little stretch of the truth, but I figured trying to explain about Skip would just be too hard.

"We wouldn't make that up," Alex said. "So, Ms. Pixman, do you have something to tell us? Maybe you need to change your story a little?"

"I don't know—" She looked away. "I don't know how my earring got down there, but I promise you, I didn't murder Nate. I *couldn't* hurt him. I may not have been in love with him like I once was in high school, but I still wouldn't want to see harm come to him." She swiped at a tear that fell from one of her eyes. "Besides, why would I report my earring stolen if I murdered Nate and then noticed it was missing? That makes zero sense."

"To cover your tracks?" Alex mused.

"I'm *not* lying," Gracie insisted.

"That's what they all say," Needles said.

"You see, Ms. Pixman," Alex said, "that might be easier for us to believe had we not already discovered you've lied to us before."

Color drained from Gracie's face. "What do you mean?"

Alex crossed his arms over his chest. "Agent Loci and I learned something interesting yesterday. You claim when you left the bar Wednesday night that Anya didn't follow you. Yet we got a different story."

Gracie closed her eyes briefly. "You're right. I didn't want to say anything because I *knew* how it would look. But I wasn't lying. I just didn't tell you everything. I honestly didn't know Anya followed me out until I got outside the front of the hotel. I thought I'd take a walk. Just let all the negativity go. But when I stepped outside, I heard Anya call my name. I had to make a snap decision. If I went right, I'd go by the lake and boat area. But that path was lit up nice and bright. I headed left around the building since it was darker. But she caught me trying to run from her."

I cocked my head. "So she caught you on the side of the building where the employee parking lot is?"

"I guess so. It happened so fast. She reached me in seconds, which wasn't surprising. She's a werewolf, and I'm a pixie. She struck me in the face, and I just lost it. I have *no* idea how to fight. I've never been in one, but I just reacted and reached for her. She did the same thing. I think maybe we ended up on the ground, pulling hair and stuff? But I don't know. When I came back to myself, I remember Mavis Firestone was there, and she had ahold of me and was telling me to take a walk and cool down. Another woman was there trying to calm Anya down."

"And what did you do?" I asked.

"I ran from there," Gracie said. "I just wanted away. I was embarrassed and humiliated to be caught fighting by a colleague and a hotel employee."

"You should have been upfront with the story," Alex said. "Because now we know you lied, and we have to wonder what else have you've lied or left out?"

Gracie shook her head and twirled the diamond bracelet on her wrist. "I haven't. I swear. I didn't kill Nate."

"I'm going to need to keep ahold of this earring for a while," I said. "We have your information."

Gracie nodded, turned, and trudged back to the elevator.

"Let's go check out where this fight happened," Alex said.

We headed out the door and took a left. At the end of the building, we took another left, and sure enough, halfway down the side was a parking lot. Ten cars were parked twenty feet or so away from the building near a dumpster.

"Notice that door?" I said. "Says 'Kitchen Staff Only' on the plate. Wanna bet that's the door that leads to the kitchen?"

Alex smiled. "Given where we're standing and where we already know the kitchen layout to be, I'd say you're exactly right."

"Something smells good." Needles poked his head out of the dumpster, and I almost gagged. *"Wanna help me find some lunch?"*

"Get out of there," I said. "That's disgusting."

"Let's go back inside and talk with Melody again," Alex said. "I want to find and talk to the two employees who saw the altercations between Anya and Gracie."

"You mean the bathroom yelling match and this parking lot fight?"

He nodded. "Yeah. We know the woman who overheard them Tuesday night in the bathroom was a server. Let's see if we can narrow down who it was. The worker who saw Wednesday's fight outside might be harder to pin. No one knew who she was or in what capacity she worked."

It didn't take long for Melody to identify the server who overheard the argument in the bathroom. As luck would have it, she was working the morning and lunch shift. Melody didn't know for sure who the employee in the parking lot had been Wednesday night, but she gave us a couple names to check. Alex and I decided to go to the bar and grab some lunch and find the server we needed to speak with.

"So, is this where you're gonna be hanging out tonight?" Alex asked as he held open one side of the door for me.

I smiled up at him. "Probably."

He grunted, and I heard Needles snickering in my ear.

We sidled up to the bar, sat down on some empty stools, and waited for the bartender to head our way. I caught the eye of the guy sitting at the bar like we were, and groaned.

Owen Oldblood.

He raised his glass to me and grinned.

"What can I get you two?" the bartender asked.

"What's your soup today?" I asked.

"Gazpacho." She smiled. "You can't go wrong with it. The tomatoes, cucumbers, zucchini, and onions are all locally grown here on the island. It's delicious."

"Sounds great," I said. "I'll take it, and just water to drink."

"Same," Alex said.

"Coming up."

"I'll see if I can hear any good gossip," Needles said as he flew toward the ceiling.

The bartender left to put in our order, and I turned on my barstool to look around the room. Gretna, the server we were looking for, strode into the bar carrying plates of food. I waited until she served her table before motioning her over.

"Yes?" Gretna asked politely. "Can I help you?"

I quickly introduced who we were, then jumped right in because she was busy. "What can you tell us about the argument you overheard in the bathroom Tuesday night?"

Gretna grimaced. "We aren't supposed to listen in on what goes on between guests." She looked around. "And I really don't want to get in trouble. I need this job. I got a kid wanting to go to college in about three years."

"It's okay," I said. "Melody is the one who told us to speak to you."

Gretna sighed. "Okay. So I don't know names, just hair color and body size. One girl was beefy and strong...the other was skinny and sweet looking. The strong girl with the brown hair was telling the skinny blonde to stop flirting with her guy. He'd never leave her. They were happy together. All that kind of talk. The blonde just looked like she wanted to bolt—I could see them through the crack in the stall. The blonde never really said anything. I stayed in the stall as long as I could, then when I couldn't take it any longer, I walked out. The small girl looked relieved. I'm pretty sure she hightailed it out right behind me." She held up her hands. "That's all I know."

"So no physical altercation?" I asked.

"Nope. Not that I saw."

"Thanks for speaking with us," Alex said.

When she left, I turned to Alex and rolled my eyes. "I told you they wouldn't talk to us openly. It's too intimidating."

"So you keep saying," Alex said.

I laughed and turned back around to face the bar. "That's why we're doing girls' night out tonight at the bar. It's Karaoke night. I bet once things get loosened up, tongues will wag."

"Did I hear you say you're singing tonight?" Owen sidled up next to me and leaned in until we were inches apart. I turned and stared at him...and felt a pull I wasn't entirely comfortable with. "Perhaps it is a good thing Jordan asked us to extend our stay another night. I cannot wait to hear your exquisite voice, Agent Loci."

I heard Alex growl...but before he could react any further, Needles flew down from the overhead rafters, a quill in each hand, yelling words I'd be grounded for if Mom ever heard—even at forty.

"That's it, Vampire," Needles threw one quill in the air above his head, twirled, then caught it midair. *"We rumble now."*

"That was actually impressive," Alex murmured.

"Don't encourage him," I hissed.

Needles' wings were glowing red, and I knew if I didn't step in, things were about to go downhill fast.

"Needles," I said, "back off now. Mr. Oldblood didn't mean anything by his comment."

I saw Owen open his mouth, and I almost let him step in it and feel Needles' wrath, but I couldn't in good conscious let that happen. "Owen, you're gonna want to keep your mouth shut right now. Needles may look small and unassuming, but he's got over two hundred years of fighting experience behind him, along with the power of my father. And trust me, that's something you don't want to mess with."

Something in my voice must have alerted Owen to the seriousness of the situation, because he raised his hands, gave me a greasy smile, and slowly backed away. "I meant no disrespect, Agent Loci." He gave me a wink. "Maybe we can take this back up later tonight."

Before I could chew him out for being an idiot, Owen disappeared from the room. He'd left so quickly, I felt a breeze.

"That was creepy," I said.

"Do all vampires move that fast?" Alex asked. "I've not experienced it before."

"Not usually," I said. "I mean, they have speed, but that was unnatural."

"He's old," Needles said as he settled back down on my shoulder. *"I could feel his power when he tried to mesmerize you. Old school practices."*

"What?" I said, totally confused.

"What's Needles saying?" Alex asked.

"Needles said he thought Owen was trying to do the old-school practice of mesmerizing me. Which makes sense. I felt this weird pull inside me I didn't like when he looked into my eyes. I guess Needles could feel how old and powerful Owen was when he did that, even though Needles wasn't near me."

"Is it dangerous?" Alex asked.

"Not really," I said. "It's just not something vampires around here do. It's not needed on Enchanted Island. That whole 'look into my eyes' thing went by the wayside centuries ago. I guess on the mainland it's still used." I shrugged. "I can see how it might be handy in his line of work. Try and get the clients to go with you by bespelling them? Seems a little unethical, but when you're dealing in only supernatural companies, maybe it's acceptable practice."

Alex frowned. "It makes me wonder what else might he do with that power?"

"Like lure someone to their death?" I mused.

"Exactly."

Chapter Seventeen

"It's the most amazing thing I've ever seen." Serena set her glass of red wine down on the table. "I can't *wait* to get married here."

"It *was* pretty spectacular," Grant agreed.

The four of us, plus Needles, were sitting out on the back patio overlooking the small pond. Serena and Grant had just finished their wedding venue tour, and Serena was celebrating with wine. I took that as a good sign.

"What was so amazing about it?" I asked. "Can you tell me? Or is it a secret?"

Serena took a sip from her glass. "First off, we've decided on a time, not so much the date yet. But I want to celebrate my dragon side—in honor of my dad—so the wedding will be at dusk, right before the sun sets. This way I can incorporate fire and red."

Serena's dad had been killed while she was still in her mom's womb nearly thirty years earlier. Most people assumed her dad went down with his ship during a storm, but recently Serena and I had discovered the truth. Her dad had been murdered.

"I think that's a wonderful tribute," I said.

"Melody can do this spell," Serena continued, "where thousands of tiny lights appear overhead. Plus, she can do them in any color. So I'm thinking red twinkling stars. How cool would that be?"

"Very cool," I said.

"Would you want an afternoon or dusk wedding?" Alex asked me. "I assume you've thought about it?"

My mouth dropped, and I made this weird gurgling sound. Serena giggled and kicked me under the table.

Alex laughed. "I didn't mean *today*. I meant in general. You've had forty years to think about it."

I laughed. "I suppose I have. Well, to be honest, I have thought about a few things I'd like."

"Like what?" Alex asked.

"First, it would have to be small and intimate because I'd want it to be in Black Forest. Second, I'd want it at night so the lightening bugs could hold my train and veil as I walk down the forest aisle. I want to see the stars overhead and smell the night forest."

Serena sighed. "I love that image. And can I steal the lightening bugs things?" She wrinkled her nose. "Only not fireflies." She gasped. "I wonder if Melody could do a spell to have butterflies carry my trail and veil?"

"Why ask Melody?" I mused. "Why not ask me?"

"You can do that?" Serena whispered.

I laughed and nodded. "I can. It's just a matter of asking them to do it. No spell needed. The animals are always glad to help."

Serena rested her hand on her chest. "I'd *love* it if a couple butterflies did that." She bit her lip. "I mean, it's not animal cruelty or anything, is it?"

Needles laughed so hard, he tipped backward off my shoulder and popped up in the air. *"She's a funny one. Animal cruelty!"*

"Needles thinks it is sweet of you to ask," I said. "Trust me, the butterflies would be happy to do it. They love that kind of stuff. In fact, they'll probably fight over who gets to do it."

"Especially if *you* ask them, Shayla," Alex said. "I've noticed that most animals want to please you."

I shuddered. "Except Wendy Wand's cats. Those things wanted to eat me!"

Serena laughed so loud, nearby guests turned to look at us.

"It's true," Serena said. "I will *never* forget how fast you came flying down that hallway telling me we needed to leave. I've never seen anything funnier."

"What about you, Grant?" I asked. "What do you visualize for your wedding?"

He grinned. "Serena and me getting hitched."

I rolled my eyes. "Obviously."

Grant shrugged. "I don't know. I really don't care. I mean, I *care*, but I don't have to have certain things. Just Serena. So whatever she wants is fine by me."

"Easy enough," I said.

Serena raised her wine glass in the air. "That's why I love him."

They leaned over and kissed.

Alex cleared his throat. "Now that we have the wedding venue taken care of, and everyone is caught up on where we are in the investigation, I suppose we should go over the background checks and discuss our suspects."

"I'll give us some privacy," I said.

I closed my eyes and whispered the spell I'd been taught that would make it so others couldn't overhear our conversation. Putting us in a bubble-like barrier. As I whispered the spell, I brought my arms up and over my head, as though sealing us inside. The instant silence from the outside world was powerful. Nothing could be heard but our breathing.

"Okay," I said. "We are free to talk."

Grant flipped open the folder in front of him. "I ran background checks on Jordan Owlman, Anya Moony, Mavis Firestone, Owen Oldblood, and Gracie Pixman. Jordan is oddly clean. I mean, not even a ticket. Anya Moony was actually brought in by Sheriff Hawkins two years ago for drunk and disorderly. Seems she got drunk down at Boos & Brews and started a fight. Spent the weekend in jail, and did a little community service."

"That's a shock," I said dryly.

Grant grinned, then picked up another sheet. "Mavis Firestone in the human courts basically has speeding and parking tickets. In the supernatural courts, she has a harassment charge *and* had a restraining order against her by a supernatural ex-boyfriend. It was two separate events that happened about seven years ago. She didn't do jail time, but she was fined about ten thousand dollars."

Serena whistled. "That's a little crazy."

Alex frowned. "I'm actually surprised she didn't do time on the harassment charge."

"Ditto." Grant withdrew another paper. "Owen Oldblood is fairly clean."

"Probably because if he was ever stopped," I said, "he just vampire hypnotized the officers into letting him go."

"What?" Serena said. "That's a thing?"

"It is with Owen," I said. "He tried to do it to me today."

"I should have plucked out his eyeballs when I had the chance."

"You're kidding!" Serena said. "And he's still alive? Needles didn't fillet him?"

I laughed. "Needles *just* said he should have plucked out his eyeballs when he had the chance."

"Here, here." Serena lifted her glass of red wine to Needles.

"Oh, to drink the blood of my enemies as she does."

I gagged. "Gross!"

"What?" Serena asked.

"Needles made a joke about how he wishes he could be like you and drink the blood of his enemies."

Serena grinned, downed the last of her red wine, then wiped her mouth with the back of her hand. "Delicious."

"Who *are* you?" Grant asked.

Serena shrugged. "I guess I'm someone who enjoys a glass of my enemy's blood."

I laughed. "Can we please get back to the last person?"

"Gracie Pixman," Grant said. "She's clean too. Human courts a couple speeding tickets. Nothing else."

"Then let's talk suspects," Alex said. "We found a diamond earring today near the initial attack where Nate was killed. We know the earring belonged to Gracie. She insists she had it on her nightstand and someone stole it out of her room, but I don't see that happening."

"Me neither," I said. "More like it fell out of her ear when she was killing and dragging Nate's body."

"Or it was planted there," Alex said.

"What?" I mused. "Where did that come from?"

"Think about it," Alex said. "Who else probably had access to that earring Wednesday night?"

Grant snapped his fingers. "Anya. The two of them got into a physical alternation. Maybe Anya grabbed hold of it during the fight."

"And let's be honest," Alex said, "of the two women, Anya is stronger. It's one thing to take Nate unaware and stab him, but someone had to get Nate onto the magic carpet. That takes strength."

"That's actually pretty good thinking," I said. "But why would Anya kill Nate? Why not kill Gracie?"

"Because we'd arrest Anya immediately," Alex said. "Everyone saw them fighting. Even unassuming Jordan knew there were problems. But by killing Nate, she can throw the suspicion. After all, three other people came to this island vying for a profitable dating app."

I nodded. "True. Plus, she can throw suspicion on Jordan because he'd now own one hundred percent of the company."

"A very profitable company," Alex said.

"So how do we break Anya's alibi?" I asked.

"I'm still thinking on that," Alex said.

Chapter Eighteen

When it was all said and done, Serena, Finn, GiGi, and I strolled inside the crowded bar around nine. I'd convinced Needles I would be safe with three supernatural women by my side. He could just relax in the room, eating salty pretzel sticks, and watching movies. He readily agreed.

GiGi had texted me earlier in the day and wanted to know where I was. She hadn't seen me drive by her place since Thursday evening. When I told her where Serena and I were staying and what we were about to do…she demanded to tag along. Which was fine. Once loosened up, GiGi could be a lot of fun.

Or so I kept telling myself.

Since Serena was booking her wedding at The Spellmoore, Melody was nice enough not to say anything about GiGi and Finn staying overnight with us in our room.

GiGi had on her "Baddest Witch in Town" t-shirt with a bohemian multi-colored skirt and green slippers. Serena wore a lovely baby doll summer dress that hit above her knees with a matching colored wedge shoe. I had on black shorts with a silver off-the-shoulder sweater and silver sandals…but the show stopper was definitely Finn. You'd think a girl with multi-colored spiked hair, face piercings, and myriad colored tattoos would be just as flamboyant in her wardrobe choices. But tonight, Finn was dressed in a midnight blue, sleeveless sheath dress that hugged her curves and showed off her tattooed buff arms. She looked fierce.

"What are we drinking tonight, ladies?" Finn asked as we sidled up to the bar and crowded two hotel guests.

"I think I'll just have red wine," Serena said.

"Me too," I said.

Finn rolled her eyes. "Red wine? Seriously? We're here to party."

I snorted. "No, we're here to question a server and see if we can gather more information against a potential suspect."

"I could go for something refreshing," GiGi said.

The bartender strolled down to us and asked for our order. Finn beat me to the punch. "We'll have a pitcher of margaritas, and a round of tequila shots."

"Right on!" GiGi exclaimed, giving Finn a fist bump.

I groaned. "I don't see this night turning out well."

Serena laughed. "At least we won't have far to walk to get back to our beds."

"I'm supposed to be working," I said.

"I got that covered too," Finn said. "I called Jordan earlier and told him we were going to be downstairs, and I asked him to come down and have a drink with us."

"You did?" I mused. "What did he say?"

I couldn't imagine the straight-laced, grief-stricken Jordan hanging out with us over drinks.

Finn's cheeks turned pink, and she gave me a sly smile. "I

DEADLY CLIENT

have a way with Jordan." She laughed. "We go back. His older sister and I were good friends growing up. She's moved away from the island, but I keep my tabs on Jordan. Plus, I work next door to his uncle in the labs."

I grinned. "And just how close of tabs are we talking?"

I wouldn't have believed it had I not seen it with my own eyes, but this time Finn full-on flushed. "Anyway, he said he'd be down around nine-thirty." She glanced at her cell phone. "Gives us about thirty minutes to find this mysterious server and question her. Oh, by the way, my cousin is working tonight."

The four of us snagged a table and sat down. There was a nice mix of vacationing supernaturals and business supernaturals sitting in the lounge. I didn't recognize anyone from the island, but I hadn't really expected to. Most locals stay in town and hit those restaurants and bars on a Friday night. Directly in front of us, across the room, was a makeshift stage and microphone. The dreaded karaoke stage.

"Your cousin?" I asked.

"Petra," Finn said. "Remember? She sometimes works the restaurant, other times works the bar. Just depends."

"That's right," I said.

"Here ya go, ladies."

I looked up and saw Finn—but in total opposite form. Instead of multi-colored spikes, she had her dark hair pulled into a messy bun on top of her head. Her face was devoid of piercings and makeup, and there wasn't a tattoo to be seen. But she looked like a carbon copy of Finn.

"Petra!" Finn cried. "I was just telling the girls you're working tonight."

Petra set down the tray and distributed our glasses, limes, and salt. "I am. And I hear the first round is shots. Nicely done, cousin. Your pitcher of margarita should be up shortly."

"Before you leave," I said. "I was wondering if you might be able to help us. It's probably a long shot, but has a staff worker mentioned seeing a fight in the employee parking lot on Wednesday night? I need to speak to that person. It's important."

Petra's eyes went wide. "You heard about that?"

"Drink your shot," GiGi said.

"I'm a little busy," I hissed.

"Drink! Drink!" Finn chanted.

Sighing, I picked up my shot glass and gulped it down. When I set the empty glass back on the table, I noticed Serena's shocked face. "What?"

"You didn't even partake of the salt and lime," Serena whined.

"I'm a little busy here," I said. "I don't have time for all that extra junk."

Petra laughed. "I like you."

"So, do you know who the worker was?" I asked.

Petra looked around the room, then leaned in close. "We aren't supposed to talk about things that go on between the guests here. Ms. Spellmoore is adamant about guest privacy."

I waved my hand in the air. "Melody knows I'm here asking. In fact, she actually gave me a list of names of the women working that night. I have it somewhere in my purse."

"It was me," Petra said. "I was in my car getting ready to leave when I saw two women fighting."

"What exactly did you see and do?" I asked.

"I heard them shouting first," Petra said. "I stepped out of my car and that's when the stockier girl hit the smaller girl. Well, maybe not hit is right. It was more the stockier girl raked her nails down the side of the smaller girl's face. By the time I ran to them, they were on the ground. I could see blood on the smaller girl's cheek. At some point, another guest ran over and helped me. She obviously knew the smaller girl because she told her to take a walk and cool off."

"So the stockier girl," I said, "she reached over and touched the smaller girl's face. You saw that?"

"Yes. And then they both just went at each other. I had to give props to the little one. She was no match for the other girl, but she tried to take her on. The older lady that came to help me, she must be a witch because she murmured a healing spell and closed the gash on the girl's cheek. As luck would have it, I had a bottled water on me I hadn't opened, so I gave it to the bleeding girl to wash up with. She took it and pretty much ran toward the back of the hotel."

"What happened next?" I asked.

"The older lady yelled at the girl who started the fight and threatened to kick her butt while holding fireballs in her hands." Petra laughed. "It was awesome, but also very weird. The fighting girl turned and went back to the front of the hotel, and I thanked the other lady for helping. She nodded and told me she'd wait for me to get in my car to make sure I was safe. So that's what I did. Got in my car and drove away."

"That's what I needed to know," I said. "Thanks for your help."

She laid a hand on Finn's shoulder. "Anytime. Let me get your next round. It should be up."

"I need to make a call to Alex real quick," I said. "I'll be back shortly."

I hurried out to the hallway where it was quieter. I could have texted him, but I wanted to hear his voice. He picked up on the second ring.

"Hey, Loci. Having fun?"

"I am actually," I said. "I mean, once I found the witness in the parking lot to Wednesday night's fight, I perked right up."

"What? You spoke to the woman who saw everything? Nice going. What did she say?"

"Pretty much what Mavis Firestone said. Anya made physical contact with the side of Gracie's face. They rolled around on the ground. So pretty much anytime during that scuffle, Anya could have snagged the earring."

"I'll pick Anya up first thing in the morning and bring her to the station for a formal interview," Alex said.

"Great. Do me a favor? Can you have Grant come out here and pick up Gracie and take her down to the station too? I don't like the fact Gracie obviously lied to us again. She said she had the earring on her bedside. We now know that's a lie. I want to know why she made a production of going down to the front lobby to make allegations against housekeeping."

"Sure thing," Alex said. "I'll have him there by eight."

"Great. I better get back inside." I paused. "Have you heard from Zoie yet?"

Alex sighed. "Not yet. She doesn't have to be home until midnight."

"I wonder if he'll kiss her goodnight?"

Alex growled. "Why did you do that?"

I laughed. "Well, gotta run. See ya in the morning, Sheriff Stone."

I disconnected…but not before I heard him swearing.

Chapter Nineteen

Two pitchers of margaritas later, karaoke going strong, and Finn constantly looking at her cell phone...Jordan Owlman finally shuffled uncertainly through the doors. He looked around the dimly lit bar, his big owl eyes blinking rapidly behind his glasses, and wiped his hands on his jeans.

"Look who just arrived," I said.

Finn's face lit up, and she bolted from our table and hurried over to Jordan. For a second, I thought he was going to bolt from the room when Finn ran toward him, but he stood his ground and greeted her. He again looked terrified as she dragged him over to our table.

"Look everyone," Finn said, "Jordan decided to join us."

We all scooted over as Petra grabbed a chair from a neighboring table and brought it over to us.

"What are you drinking?" Petra asked. "Margaritas like the ladies? Or maybe a beer?"

Jordan cleared his throat. "I think I'll just have a beer. Whatever you have on tap is fine."

When Petra turned to leave, Finn patted Jordan's hand. "I thought maybe you'd changed your mind and wouldn't come at all."

Jordan gave her a little smile. "Honestly? I thought about it. I'm never comfortable in situations like this, but add to it that I feel guilty having a good time when Nate has died." He shrugged. "It just didn't feel right. But then Uncle Gordon called. I asked his opinion, and he said I should go."

"I'm glad you're here," Finn said.

"Me too."

Petra set down a mug of beer and hurried off to help another customer.

Jordan cleared his throat. "You look awful pretty tonight, Finn. That blue dress really brings out your tattoos."

I picked up my glass and downed it before I could laugh out loud and hurt Jordan's feelings. GiGi wasn't so nice. She cackled and lifted her glass of margarita in the air. "I like you, Jordan. It's always the quiet ones you have to watch out for."

"I'll drink to that!" Finn laughed.

Serena met my eyes over her glass, and I could tell she was enjoying herself as much as I was. We were an eclectic group… but we were a fun group.

I was just about as relaxed as a person could get—having guzzled down three glasses of margaritas—when Owen Oldblood and Mavis Firestone strolled through the lounge doors. I sat up straighter in my chair.

I probably shouldn't have been surprised to see them. Jordan had told us earlier he'd decided on a company to sell the app to, and he would make the announcement tomorrow around two in the conference room. So they had one more night to blow off some steam before heading back to the mainland and back to their jobs.

"Petra is busy." I snatched up our empty basket of pretzels. "I'll just go see if the bartender won't fill this for us real quick."

"I'll go with you," Jordan said, his face flushed. "I could use another beer."

"Let's go," I said.

We'd no sooner leaned against the bar when Owen flanked me on my left and Mavis flanked Jordan on his right. I handed the basket to the bartender and asked for a refill while Jordan ordered another beer.

"I'm glad to see you here tonight," Owen crooned. "Have you and your friends started singing?"

Now that I knew Owen wasn't above using hypnotic tactics, I looked just over his shoulder when I answered. "Nope. And we don't plan on singing."

"Is that so?" Owen smirked. "I guess they didn't get the memo."

I heard the amusement in Owen's voice and turned to see what he meant. Sure enough, GiGi and Finn all but ran to the table that held the book of songs. I closed my eyes and groaned. We'd officially had too much to drink if GiGi and Finn were ready to sing in public.

The bartender handed me the pretzels and slid the beer in front of Jordan. I turned to leave...and noticed Jordan didn't follow.

"He'll be along shortly, dear," Mavis said to me.

I looked at the wide-eyed Jordan and frowned. "I think we go on next to sing, Mavis. And he's our tenor."

Jordan made a move to stand, but Mavis laughed and rested both hands on Jordan's arm, locking him in place. "Then I'll make sure what I have to say is quick."

There wasn't much more I could do that wouldn't cause a scene. With a nod to Mavis, and a cold shoulder to Owen, I hurried back over to our table. "Jordan may need a save in a minute."

Finn glanced at the bar and scowled. Mavis was now inches from Jordan's face, and her hands were on his shoulder and arm.

"Is she hitting on him?" Serena asked.

"That cougar!" Finn exclaimed.

"Actually," I said, "she's just a fire elemental witch." I grinned at Serena. "Like you, Serena, she likes fire."

Serena gasped. "She's *nothing* like me."

"She's about to be toast," Finn said. "It's times like this I wish I could do magic. I'd do a little zap on her poaching butt."

"Allow me," Gigi said.

I shook my head. "GiGi, no."

But it was too late. The air in the room suddenly took on an electric charge. I was surprised I didn't hear the sizzle and pop it was that intense. GiGi circled her hands low and slow, inches above our tabletop. When she had just the right momentum...she pushed her hands out, along with her energy.

Mavis let out a little scream, and the room fell instantly silent of laughter and talking. Even the karaoke singers had stopped singing. I bit my lip to keep from laughing while Serena grabbed her glass and drank. Mavis looked around the room, and when her eyes fell on our table, she narrowed them on GiGi.

In true GiGi fashion, she lifted her full glass of margarita in the air and saluted Mavis, cackled, then downed a huge portion of her drink.

"I'll go rescue him," Finn said. "And thanks, GiGi. That meant a lot."

Chapter Twenty

By the time I walked into the sheriff's office the next morning, it was nearing eight-thirty. Serena had gotten up at four to leave—how she managed, I have no idea. We didn't get to bed until after midnight. Once Jordan left, Finn let her hair down even more and she and GiGi spent the rest of the night doing shots and singing karaoke. Serena and I had to physically drag them away from the stage when the bar closed at midnight.

Since GiGi and Finn weren't on the clock with a job, they elected to stay at the hotel and sleep. I convinced Needles to stay behind and look after them while I drove into town. After a quick pit stop at the bakery for caffeine and sugar, I was almost back to being a full witch.

"Look what the cat dragged in," Opal said from behind her desk. "I heard you, your granny, Serena, and Finn made quite the impression out at The Spellmoore. Who knew y'all could sing like that?"

I groaned. "Who told you?"

"Told me?" Opal cackled. "Girl, I saw it all on Supernatural-

Tube. You girls have like a thousand hits so far! Your granny is the talk of the supernatural internet."

I buried my face in my hands and walked toward Alex's office. SupernaturalTube was the paranormal equivalent to YouTube. The last thing I needed was for GiGi to be an internet sensation. She'd be even harder to live with than she was already.

"Are you alive?" Alex asked when I opened his door. "Because I've seen the videos, and I wasn't sure you were even going to make it in today."

"Shut up," I growled. "Remind me to never go out with Finn and GiGi again."

Alex laughed. "It looks like you guys had a great time."

"I'm barely alive. I don't know how Serena got up to go to work at four."

Alex laughed. "Because we're in our forties. We aren't supposed to have the stamina Serena and Finn have."

"What's GiGi's excuse? She's like in her mid-eighties!"

Alex shook his head and took a sip of his coffee. "I have no idea. I just assume she puts something witchy in her coffee."

I laughed. "Probably does."

"I decided to play this a different way," Alex said. "I called in Deputy Sparks to pick up Gracie while Grant picked up Anya. I wanted us both to be here when the two ladies were brought in. They will see each other, and we can gauge their reactions."

"How long until they get here?" I asked.

"Minutes."

Alex's cell phone dinged, and he picked up his phone. "They're both in the parking lot now. Let's go observe."

And what a crazy show it was. Grant strolled in first, with Anya in handcuffs. She was spitting mad and threatening everyone. Right behind them were Sparks and Gracie. Unlike Anya, Gracie was meek with quiet tears rolling down her face.

Alex's cell went off again. He picked it up and grinned. "Yes! The warrant for Anya's clothes she wore the night of the fight and Nate's murder just came in. We are good to go."

"Want me to call Finn and have her come in?" I asked.

Alex nodded. "Yeah. Better you than me. From the looks of her last night on SupernaturalTube, she probably isn't moving very fast this morning."

"You'd be right."

I placed a quick call to Finn and was surprised to hear she was up and about to jump in the shower. She assured me she could be in her lab within the hour.

"Let's hear what the girls have to say," Alex said.

We interviewed Anya first. She was sitting impatiently at the table. The minute we walked inside the room, I could feel her anger.

"Save your speech," she said. "I know I can have an attorney present, but I don't want one, nor do I need one. This is absolutely ridiculous. You have *no right* to drag me from my house and haul me down here."

"Actually," Alex said, "we have every right. We are on the record, so I'll ask again if you want an attorney?"

"No, I don't want an attorney."

Alex nodded. "Okay. Let's just jump right in. We have three witnesses stating you and Gracie Pixman had an altercation in the employee parking lot on Wednesday night. Can you confirm that allegation?"

Anya sighed. "Yes. It happened. I caught up to her in a parking lot. We had words. She said something that made me mad, so I struck her in anger. She then accosted me and we struggled. Two women broke us up. One of them sent Gracie on her way to cry in private. I went back inside. No big deal."

Just hearing Anya's version of what happened pissed me off. "So you are admitting to striking Gracie in the face? Was it a punch or what, exactly?"

Anya huffed. "I'm sure you know by now I raked my nails down her face."

I nodded. "The basic ear-to-mouth sort of move?"

Anya shrugged. "I guess."

"What were you wearing Wednesday night?" Alex asked.

"I don't know. Pants and a shirt."

"Can you be a little more specific?" he prompted.

"Black pants and red short-sleeved shirt."

"Have you washed them?" Alex asked. "Or taken them to the dry cleaners?"

"Laundry is on Sunday," Anya said. "So they're still in my hamper. Why?"

"Great." Alex handed her a sheet of paper. "This is a warrant to search your house and retrieve those items of clothing."

"What? Why?" Anya demanded.

"To check for blood," Alex said.

"I already told you Gracie and I got into a fight."

Alex smiled and stood. "I never said I was looking for Gracie's blood."

* * *

"Good morning, Ms. Pixman," Alex said as we entered the second interview room. "I hope we didn't keep you waiting too long."

"I just don't understand what you need from me," Gracie said. "I've told you everything I know about Nate's death."

"I just have one question," I said, sitting down across from her. "I can't figure out the earring thing. Why would you lie? Why go down to the front desk Thursday morning and make such a big deal out of the fact you lost the earring?"

Gracie shrugged. "I don't know."

"You don't know?" I said. "That's strange. Because all I can think of, is that you needed an excuse if the earring was found. What happened? You returned to your room Wednesday night and discovered the earring missing? Did you panic? Maybe you worried it came off when you were moving Nate's body after you killed him?"

Gracie gasped. "No! I didn't kill Nate!"

I shrugged. "Then why lie and made a big production about the earring?"

Gracie turned her head and didn't say anything.

"Agent Loci asked you a question," Alex said.

Gracie sighed and turned back to us. "I lied because I was too embarrassed to say I might have lost it in the parking lot during a fight." A tear trailed down her cheek. "I hoped if someone found it, they might turn it in. I'm guilty of lying, not of murder."

"So you keep reminding us," Alex said.

Chapter Twenty-One

"Nothing?" Alex demanded. "You're sure?" Alex held up his hand. "I'm sorry, Finn. Of course you're sure. I just thought we'd find trace amounts of blood on Anya's clothing."

"Me too," Finn said, pushing back from her work space.

"So now what?" I asked.

Alex sighed and looked at his watch. "What a mess. It's eleven now. Jordan is making his announcement about who will get control of his app at two. After that, three of our suspects will leave the island."

"We still have three hours," I said. "Surely we can figure this out."

"What about getting a warrant for Gracie's clothes?" Finn asked.

Alex ran his hands over his face. "I can't believe I'm saying this, but I need to take an hour's personal time. I'm picking up Zoie early from the bakery today. When I made the appointment a couple weeks ago for a Saturday, I had no idea we'd be in the middle of a case."

"Is everything okay?" I asked.

"Yes." Alex sighed. "And the more I think about it, the more I think I should cancel the appointment. Zoie will understand."

"What's the appointment for?" I asked.

"Her skin. She's a little freaked about her skin hardening when she shifts into a gargoyle. I'm just making sure we don't need to do anything special for her." He shrugged. "I mean, I have guy skin. I also could shift from birth. I can't remember a time when my skin didn't harden when I turned into a gargoyle. But this is new for Zoie, and I don't know the first thing about soft teenage girl skin."

I laughed. "Spoken like a true dad."

"Very funny." He shoved his hands in his pockets. "I shouldn't be but an hour, maybe an hour and a half."

"Go!" Finn and I both said.

"We got it handled here," I added. "In fact, I think I'm going to go back out to The Spellmoore."

"Probably a good idea," Finn said. "When I left, it was just Needles and GiGi in the room. They were eyeing each other pretty seriously."

I laughed. "I better go rescue one of them from the other." I turned to Alex. "You and Zoie come out to The Spellmoore when you're finished."

"I'll be back as fast as I can," Alex promised.

When the door to Finn's lab closed, I turned to her and grinned. "I have an idea."

"I'm all ears."

"Do you know Gracie Pixman?" I asked. "I mean, did you know her when she was younger and living on the island? Or maybe saw her at fairy or pixie events?"

Finn grimaced. "Not really. That whole group was a couple years younger than me, which is why I'm afraid Jordan might think it's creepy I'm hitting on him." Finn shrugged. "But I like him. What can I say? As far as Gracie goes? I could probably get a foot in the door with her by mentioning our fae background. Why?"

"Gracie wasn't at the bar last night for you to see," I said, "but every time I've spoken with her, she's always wearing the same bracelet. She even had it on this morning at the station." I lifted an eyebrow. "I wonder if there's a spec of blood on that bracelet?"

Finn nodded. "I like it. But how do you suggest we find out? We don't have a warrant."

I grinned. "You're going to show Gracie what you do for a living now. You know, from one fae to another."

"Whaddya mean?"

"I'll explain on the way. Grab your field kit, we're gonna go gather some evidence."

* * *

Twenty minutes later, Finn knocked on Gracie's hotel door. When she saw Finn and me standing there, she groaned.

"Haven't I been subjected to enough?" Gracie asked. "What more do you want from me? I've been humiliated by my colleagues and the police, I've lost a dear childhood friend, and I'm pretty sure I lost the Super Single account. Can I just pack in peace?"

Finn stuck out her hand. "You probably don't remember me. But Jordan's older sister and I were best friends growing up. My name's Finn Faeton."

Gracie frowned and narrowed her eyes at Gracie, as though

trying to place her in her memories. "Yes. Maybe I remember you."

Finn smiled. "I was wondering if I could come in a second?"

The minute Gracie opened her mouth, I knew she was going to say no. So I beat her to the punch. "Gracie? Can I use your restroom, please? I won't be long. I promise."

Gracie sighed and stepped back, motioning us in. As she did, the diamond bracelet on her wrist twinkled. "Please hurry. Bathroom is through that door over there."

I barely contained my excitement when I noticed the drapes were drawn. That meant when I used my magic to turn off the lights, the room would be plunged into total darkness.

I gave Finn a nod and hurried toward the bathroom. I stepped inside and left the door cracked so I could overhear the conversation. When I heard Finn say the magic words, I had to be ready to spring into action.

"It's actually quite amazing," Finn said. "I just take out the luminol and spray it where I think blood might be, and then when it's pitch black, the luminol will glow if it finds something."

At the words "pitch black," I stepped out of the bathroom and waved my hand toward the light switch. The room instantly went dark. I waited to hear Finn's cry of triumph that she'd discovered blood on Gracie's bracelet…but it was eerily silent in the room.

Something wasn't right.

"Uh, so that's it," Finn said brightly. "Now you know what I do for a living."

I waved my hands again, and this time I turned on the lights. Gracie was standing with her hands on her hips, daggers shooting from her eyes.

"Get out," she gritted. "And don't even think about returning."

Chapter Twenty-Two

※

"I still don't understand how we got it so wrong?" I sat down on the edge of the hotel bed. "I thought for sure we'd find blood."

"Me too," Finn said.

Needles hugged his belly and rolled back and forth on the chair cushion. He'd been laughing hysterically ever since I started telling him what happened. *"I wish I could have seen the look on your face, Princess."*

"It wasn't *that* funny, Needles," I growled.

"Oh, but it is, Princess." His wings shimmered yellow and gold. *"Rarely do you make that big of a blunder."*

"Where's GiGi?" I asked.

"The wicked witch said she needed to go home," Needles said as he shot up off the cushion and perched on the armrest. *"Something about voting for a witch board tonight."*

"That's right," I said. "Each coven on the island is going to vote for one of their members to represent them in a collective board. That came about because of what happened a few weeks back with Tamara and Hildegard Broomington."

"Will you vote?" Finn asked.

"Yes. I'd forgotten all about it."

"So now what?" Finn asked.

"I honestly don't know," I said.

"We can go look at the crime scene again," Needles suggested.

"Needles thinks we should go look at the crime scene again," I said.

Finn snorted. "Which one? The one in the woods where he was stabbed? The shed where the magic carpets are kept? Actually, yeah, let's do that one. You guys brought the sample to me. Maybe I can find something else on the carpet."

I stood and grinned. "You just want to see the magic carpets."

She picked up her field kit and grinned back at me. "You're right."

* * *

"So the earring was found through those trees over there?" Finn asked.

We'd reached the end of the sidewalk. Right took us to the forested area, straight brought us up against the huge rocks trying to keep people out of the north side of the island, and left took us toward the golf range.

"Yep. But we found the magic carpets first." I turned left, and we strolled toward the shed. "It was actually Needles who discovered the original stabbing site."

"That's true," Needles said, fluttering between Finn and me. *"You should think about giving me a raise, Princess."*

When we reached the shed, all the bays were closed and

taped off, along with the door. I waved my hand in front of the crime scene tape at the door, and the tape stretched enough for us to duck inside before snapping back into place.

"Need me to conjure a light orb?" I asked. "It's pretty dark in here."

"Sure," Finn said. "Then you can just extinguish it after I spray the carpet with the luminol. Wait? You remember what carpet you found the sample on, right?"

"Yep. Right over here."

I whispered one of the first spells GiGi and Mom taught me when I was just a little witch. A few seconds later, I tossed the ball in the air to help light our way.

"This one's it," I said. "I recognize the pattern—you can see each is just a fraction different."

Finn set her kit down and took out the supplies she'd need. Needles zipped past us and hovered above the magic carpet Finn was about to check.

"This is it!" His wings shimmered bright red in the dimly lit room. *"This one! I know who it is! The smell!"*

"What are you talking about, Needles?" I asked.

Finn looked up from the ground. "What's going on?"

Needles did two somersaults in the air. *"I know who the killer is. Get Alex on the phone now, Princess!"*

Knowing my cell phone wouldn't get a connection inside the shed, I grabbed Finn and hauled her outside. "Needles is going crazy in there. He says he knows who the killer is. I need to call Alex."

"Who is it?" Finn asked.

I shook my head and walked off the path to get a signal. "No idea. I just did as he said and ran out here to get Alex." I held the phone up and continued walking a couple more steps. "Got it!"

I pulled up Alex's number and Zoie immediately answered.

"You're on speakerphone, Shayla. Good timing. Dad and I are about five minutes out from The Spellmoore. We should be—"

"Zoie!" I interrupted. "Tell your dad I know who the killer is. Or rather, Needles knows who the killer is."

"Who?" Alex demanded.

"Hang it up," the voice behind me said. "Or I slice her throat right here."

I slowly turned and saw Nate's killer holding a knife against Finn's throat.

Chapter Twenty-Three

"Now, where is your little flying friend?" Mavis asked. "Since you just announced he's the one who solved this little mystery."

"I don't know," I said truthfully.

"C'mon out, winged beast." Mavis applied enough pressure to the knife against Finn's neck that it drew blood, and Finn let out a little yelp.

Needles shot out of the barn, his wings glowing so red they seemed black. I also knew that look on his face. He was angry enough to take on an army single-handedly.

"Needles, wait," I said. "I need answers. Then we can take her in."

Mavis laughed. "You are one measly little witch. I can swat you both away like a pesky fly. Just like I did that idiot Nate."

"Tell me what happened," I urged. "Why did you kill him?"

"After my presentation pitch Wednesday night, I knew he would sign with Gracie's company. It was obvious even during

DEADLY CLIENT

my presentation he was just humoring me. I'll admit, I first thought to take out Gracie. Eliminate the competition. I was sure I could make it look like an accident since she and Anya were fighting. But then I was handed a gift."

"The fight in the parking lot?" I guessed.

"Yes. After everyone had left, I saw Gracie's earring on the ground and knew what I had to do. I'd kill Nate and set it up where Gracie would take the fall. Then the choice would be between that ridiculous oaf Owen and me."

"How did you get the knife from the kitchen?" I asked. "And why a knife?"

"That's easy—Gracie and Owen can't do magic. So I had to kill Nate in a way that didn't use it. As I picked the earring up off the ground, another worker came out of the kitchen staff door. He must have forgotten something because he turned back around and went inside. No key needed."

I nodded. "And if you read the menu in your room—which I know you did because you mentioned ordering room service—you would have seen where the kitchen closed around nine on weekdays."

"Correct. So I went to the back patio and sat outside until around eleven. Once I was sure the kitchen was closed down and the workers gone, I walked to the outside door, checked the door, then slipped inside. I found a knife right by the door, grabbed it, stepped back out into the parking lot, then went around back by the patio and entered the hotel that way."

I frowned. "And then what? You went upstairs and lured Nate out here with that note we found in his room?"

"Yes. I stood outside his suite door on my cell phone, rang his room phone, pretended to be a crying Gracie, then hung up. I immediately knocked on his door and slipped the note underneath, knowing he'd think it was from Gracie. When he finally arrived down here by the rocks, I hit him with a sleeping spell. This way, if anyone saw us—which I didn't think would happen that late at night—people would just think we were two drunk guests trying to walk it off. I led him off the path, stabbed him, dropped the earring by the blood, then hefted him onto the magic carpet I'd stashed nearby. Once we were on, I had the carpet fly to the edge of the property line by the river."

"I thought you said you didn't do the tour with the magic carpet ride because you like to walk," I said. "How did you know about the river?"

Mavis snorted. "Seriously? I lied. Of course I took a tour around the property. That's how I knew the river would be a great place to dump him over the side. I didn't want to make it too easy on the police and have Nate found with the bloodstain and the earring right next to it. Might be too perfect of a setup."

I met Finn's eyes and was pleased to see she was calm. "But how would killing Nate guarantee you the account?"

Mavis snorted. "Because left between me and Owen…I knew it would be me. Especially since I've been using a manipulation spell on Jordan every chance I get." She scowled. "Which is why I didn't appreciate that little trick your grandmother did last night." She took a step backward and dragged Finn with her inside the shed. "Stay back!"

"I'll try and head them off at the river," Needles said.

I waited until Mavis and Finn were inside one of the bays before hurrying after them. I came to a stop when I spotted them.

"But now you've ruined everything." Mavis pushed Finn onto a magic carpet. "I'm taking this freak of a fairy with me as insurance. There are thousands of boats available. I want one sent to the north side of the island. Ever since I stepped foot on the island, everyone says the north side is isolated and no one can go there."

"You realize the length of the island is like sixty miles, right?" I asked. "And that's just a guess on my part. No one really knows because it constantly changes. How the heck are you going to find this boat? Also, I can guarantee you it won't happen. The minute you try and cross over the river into the north section of the woods, you're done. You'll be struck down."

"We'll just see about that," Mavis smirked. "Forward!"

The magic carpet came to life and lifted both Mavis and Finn in the air. A second later, the two were out of the shed and heading toward the property line.

I dropped onto the nearest carpet and tried to remember what Melody told me about the steering of the carpet. I could do it verbally or with my mind. The carpet's magic understood both.

"Forward!" I yelled.

I barely contained my scream as the carpet lifted, then shot out the door behind Mavis. Well, maybe "shot" was a little strong. It was more like the carpet tootled after Mavis, but it was still a surprise.

As both carpets hurried to the edge of the property line where the river began, I could just make out Needles hovering directly in our path. He had a quill in each paw and a look of determination on his face. I was about to scream for him to move when he shot up straight in the air and let Mavis fly by him over the river to the other side where the pine trees stood guard.

I hurried my rug over to him. "What's going on?"

"I made contact with Black Forest King. He will not allow Mavis passage into the northern territory. Instead, he will lead her carpet down the river toward the waterfall and geyser. He has alerted the forest and animals of the danger, and they are standing by ready to help you."

"Why can't I pass through these darn trees?" Mavis screamed.

A pine tree whipped out a branch and struck Mavis in the face, knocking her on her butt. She quickly sprang up from the carpet and hurled a burst of fire at the tree. I could hear the cries of pain from the old pine…but before I could think of what to do, a giant stream of water shot up from the river and put out the fire.

"She has no idea what she's doing," Needles said. *"She doesn't understand what Black Forest is."*

I gasped when Finn stood up and tried to grab the knife from Mavis. The two grappled and struggled for a few seconds before Mavis got the upper hand and pushed Finn over the carpet…and down onto the rocky river bottom below.

I screamed as Finn disappear. I was barely aware of Mavis yelling curse words as her magic carpet moved down the river toward the waterfall. I guided my carpet over the river until I could see Finn. Her mangled body lay face-down on the rocks, inches from the swirling river.

"Stay with her!" I yelled to Needles. "I mean it! Keep her alive! Tell Alex I'm going after Mavis."

"I will. Black Forest King is leading Mavis' carpet to the geyser. He said he has every confidence you can take it from there."

"Damn right I will," I growled.

I chased Mavis' carpet down the river. I could hear her screams of frustration as she tried to stop the carpet. When that didn't work, she threw fire at everything around her in a fit of anger. But she was no match for the river. Every time a fireball landed on the grassy embankment, the river retaliated by sending a wave to put it out.

I smiled as Mavis' magic carpet plummeted quickly over the waterfall, and she screamed in terror all the way down. My magic carpet was gentler and glided me over the falls and down toward the flat clearing near the edge of the river and the geyser.

When Mavis' carpet bucked her off, and she went flying through the air before toppling to the ground, I couldn't help myself...I laughed out loud. My carpet came to rest, and I quickly stepped off.

"It's over, Mavis," I yelled. "Give it up. Black Forest King will never let you out of here alive if you don't surrender to me."

"I'm not scared of you!" Mavis yelled as she picked herself up off the ground. "Or any Black Forest King. Whatever that is."

My hand hovered above the binder on my belt. I just needed to get a little closer, and I could release the binder and capture her alive.

Mavis lifted her arms in the air and gathered energy between her palms. "You think you scare me? I've been practicing magic longer than you've been alive. I'm going to crush you."

She sent a stream of fire my way, and once again, the river interceded on my behalf and doused the flames before they could even reach me. I laughed at the frustration on her face.

A growl to our right had us both turning our heads. Two wolves stood side-by-side each other, lips curled back over their sharp teeth. Behind them were countless deer, rabbits, squirrels, and other forest animals.

"It ends here." I lowered my hand off the binder and slowly raised my hands, palms up. The leaves and twigs on the ground swirled around me like a vortex the higher my arms raised in the air. "The flora and the fauna do as I ask, Mavis Firestone." It was all I could do to contain the powerful energy running through my body. "One word from me and you will be no more. But I will give you this chance. Surrender, and I will let you live."

"Never!"

She raised her hands to blast me again...but she never got the chance. I hurled my mass of energy at her chest, knocking her backward a good five feet in the air. She landed on her back on top of the geyser. Dazed, she shook her head and tried to stand. The forest floor shook, causing Mavis to fall again. A few seconds later, steam erupted from the geyser, cutting off her screams. By the time the water finished spraying in the air... Mavis Firestone was dead.

Chapter Twenty-Four

I left Mavis where she was and hopped back on the magic carpet. I needed to see about Finn. I urged the carpet up and over the waterfall and down the riverbed. I could feel the tears rolling down my cheeks, and I didn't try to stop them. I knew there was no way Finn survived that fall.

By the time I reached Finn's body, Alex, Zoie, and Needles were kneeling over her, and Alex and Zoie had both shifted into gargoyles.

"She's bad," Alex said, his voice rough and gravely. "I called for an ambulance, but I'm not sure if they'll make it here in time. Zoie and I had to fly down here just to reach her."

I finally swiped away my tears. I didn't have time for them right now. "Needles? Ask Dad what I should do."

"I already have, Princess. He said you must call GiGi and get her to ride her Vespa out to the entrance of Black Forest. She has permission to enter. She is the only witch powerful enough to do what must be done as quickly as it must be done. We can't wait for your mom to get there. Have GiGi bring a cauldron."

"GiGi isn't going to—"

"*Tell her it's a matter of life or death for your friend,*" Needles interrupted. "*She must do this! Zoie, tell your dad to fly Finn to Black Forest King. After Shayla has spoken to GiGi, you both need to fly to Black Forest. Do you think you can fly Shayla there, Zoie?*"

"Yes," Zoie said.

"Yes what?" Alex demanded. "I hate not being in the loop."

I quickly filled him in on what Needles said. Alex gently picked up Finn and shot off into the sky with her, not even bothering to question anything. I dug my cell phone out of my pocket and phoned GiGi.

"Where are you?" I demanded. "Are you home? This is important."

"I'm at home, child," GiGi said. "Where are you?"

"At The Spellmoore. There's been a horrible accident, GiGi. It's Finn." I cleared my throat when a sob tried to break through. "Black Forest King said you need to ride your Vespa down the path behind my house and the pines will let you inside Black Forest."

Silence. "I'm not entering Black Forest, Shayla."

"GiGi! He said you are the only witch powerful enough on the island to do what needs done. You and Dad must put aside your differences right now. I need you! Finn needs you! She will *die* if you don't help her." I could hear the panic in my voice. "She was only helping me in the investigation, and I got her killed. Please, GiGi. If you can't do this for Dad, please do it for me and Finn."

GiGi sighed. "I can be there in about five minutes. That's the fastest the Vespa can go."

"Thank you! Zoie is flying me there now. We'll meet you at the entrance."

I disconnected, then turned to Zoie. "Ready?"

"I'm a little scared," Zoie said, her deep voice shaking. "I don't want to drop you."

I rested my hands on her shoulders. "I trust you, Zoie. You got this." I motioned for Needles to nestle close to my neck and hang on. There was no way his wings could keep up with Zoie, no matter how much he teased her otherwise. "How do you want to carry me?"

Zoie laughed. "I guess like a new bride? It's so odd how strong I am in this form. I can't get over it."

I raised my arms high. "Like a bride it is."

***

When Alex first laid Finn at the base of Dad's trunk, she had massive internal bleeding, a broken pelvis, leg, arm, and collar bone. I didn't think there was any way she would live.

But I was wrong.

"Here's the last of the ingredients." Needles dropped the flower in GiGi's cauldron.

"Thank you," GiGi closed her eyes and started to whisper the spell.

"Alex," Dad said, *"Finn will feel this even in her unconscious state. Please hold her down as gently as you can. GiGi will pour the spelled liquid down her throat while I heal her. But we need to hurry."*

I stood near the base of the tree, holding Zoie's hand. Finn's broken body looked pale and fragile lying on the ground. When the liquid in GiGi's cauldron burned out, she poured it into a chalice and went to stand next to Alex.

"Daughter, since you are a part of me, you will feel this too. If you don't want to stay, I understand."

"Of course I want to stay," I said. "I want to be here for Finn. Will it hurt?"

"No," Dad said. *"In fact, pulling from your essence will actually help."*

I'm not sure what my dad did, but I felt it immediately. He was right, it didn't exactly hurt…more like my insides were tingling. A brilliant white light shot up from the base of Dad's tree, and both Alex and GiGi had to avert their eyes. I could see the agony on Alex's face as he tried to hold Finn down and calm her, but it was no use. She thrashed and cried out. When the bright light diminished, GiGi's quickly poured the liquid down Finn's throat. It wasn't until Finn was all cried out that Zoie let go of the death grip she had on my hand.

When it was all said and done, Finn looked nothing like the broken and twisted girl she had been just minutes before. Her leg and arm were straight. I assumed her pelvis and collar bone were fixed as well.

"The bleeding inside has been repaired," Dad said. *"She will need a few days to recover, but should be back to her old self by the end of the week."*

"How did you do it?" I whispered.

"All in due time, Daughter of my Heart," Dad said. *"Thank you, GiGi, for your help."*

"You're welcome," GiGi said.

And the crazy thing was…she looked like she meant it.

"Your mother just entered Black Forest, Shayla," Dad said.

GiGi grunted, but didn't say anything.

"Should I take Finn to the hospital?" Alex asked.

"*You can,*" Dad said. "*Everything is set perfectly, but they may want to see her.*"

Alex grinned. "I have no doubt you healed her completely. I just didn't know if I was to take her home or to the hospital."

"*I am not insulted, Shayla's young man,*" Dad said. "*It was a noble question.*"

"I got here as fast as I could," Mom said as she burst through the clearing. "Is there anything I can do?"

"*We just finished,*" Dad said. "*GiGi was a tremendous help, Serenity. I could not have asked for a better partner. Or rather, Finn could not have asked for better help.*"

"I think I'm going to get Finn to the hospital," Alex said. "Zoie? You ready?"

Zoie gave me a quick hug. "I am."

"I'll call you later tonight," Alex said as he kissed my cheek. "What should we do about Mavis' body?"

"*If you'd like,*" Dad said, "*I can get word to Dr. Marcus Drago and have him retrieve her body in his dragon form.*"

"That would be helpful," Alex said. "If you're sure you are okay with him in that location."

Dad chuckled. "*The Dragos are trustworthy and will always be considered family. I trust Dr. Drago with this task.*"

Alex shifted into his gargoyle form, scooped the still-unconscious Finn up in his arms, and patiently waited for Zoie to shift before the two of them flew off into the night sky.

"Sounds like I missed a lot," Mom said, laying a hand on Dad's trunk. "Thank you for helping Shayla's friend."

"*I'm glad I could help.*"

"Well, I better be off," GiGi said. "Don't forget, Shayla, you need to drive into town later and cast your vote for our coven meeting tonight. All the covens around the island are meeting and voting on the special board we are forming. This is an important election for every witch on the island."

I groaned. "I'm exhausted."

"It's your duty," GiGi snapped. "This family is one of the few founding members left on Enchanted Island, and your father is Black Forest King, for goodness' sake. You have a duty and an obligation to the island, Shayla. Remember that."

Without another word, GiGi turned and stalked out of the forest.

We were all momentarily stunned.

"That's the first time," Mom said, "GiGi has ever acknowledged your birthright, Shayla, from *both* sides of the tree."

I snickered. "Nice pun, Mom."

Mom and Dad both chuckled.

But it was true. GiGi never spoke kindly about my dad, and she definitely never acknowledged everything he represented about Enchanted Island. This was a big deal.

"Well," I said, "I guess I better get home and get ready. Mom, you coming?"

Mom cleared her throat and looked up at Dad. "I was thinking maybe I'll stay a little longer. If that's okay?"

"My dearest, Serenity, you are always welcome. While Black Forest is my heart and soul. Having you here makes my heart happy and full."

I smiled at that. I always said Black Forest brought me comfort and peace the moment I stepped inside…and here was Dad, telling Mom she brought *him* happiness and peace when she stepped inside Black Forest. Their love for each other was still strong even after all these years.

"Needles? Do me a favor and stay with Mom," I said. "It's still light enough for me to see. Mom, take your time. I'll see you tonight at the coven meeting."

As I jogged through Black Forest, I couldn't help but wonder about the new board being elected. I wanted to be optimistic, but I wasn't sure what this change would mean for the witches on Enchanted Island.

* * *

Ready for Book 8, Deadly Coven? Click here: My Book It's the night of the new coven board meeting… and a witch has just dropped dead in front of Shayla.

* * *

Do you love the idea of a time-traveling, cold-case solving witch? Then Lexi and her side-kick detective familiar, Rex the Rat, are just what you're looking for! Check out their first stop to 1988 in Time After Time My Book

Have you read the hilarious adventures of Ryli Sinclair and Aunt Shirley? Book 1 is Picture Perfect Murder! My Book

Love the idea of a bookstore/bar set in the picturesque wine country of Sonoma County? Then join Jaycee, Jax, Gramps, Tillie, and the whole gang as they solve murders while slinging suds and chasing bad guys in this hilarious series. My Book

. . .

How about a seaside mystery? My stepdaughter and I write a mystery where high school seniors pair up with their grandma and great-aunt! Book one, Seaside & Homicide: My Book

Or maybe you're in the mood for a romantic comedy…heavy on comedy and light on sweet romance? Then the Trinity Falls series is for you! My Book

Looking for a paranormal cozy series about a midlife witch looking to make a new start with a new career? Then A Witch in the Woods is the book series for you! A game warden witch, a talking/flying porcupine, and a gargoyle sheriff! My Book

About the Author

Jenna writes in the genres of cozy/paranormal cozy/ romantic comedy. Her humorous characters and stories revolve around over-the-top family members, creative murders, and there's always a positive element of the military in her stories. Jenna currently lives in Missouri with her fiancé, step-daughter, Nova Scotia duck tolling retriever dog, Brownie, and her tuxedo-cat, Whiskey. She is a former court reporter turned educator turned full-time writer. She has a Master's degree in Special Education, and an Education Specialist degree in Curriculum and Instruction. She also spent twelve years in full-time ministry.

When she's not writing, Jenna likes to attend beer and wine tastings, go antiquing, visit craft festivals, and spend time with her family and friends. Check out her website at http://www.jennastjames.com/. Don't forget to sign up for the newsletter so you can keep up with the latest releases! You can also friend request her on Facebook at jennastjamesauthor/ or catch her on Instagram at authorjennastjames.

Printed in Dunstable, United Kingdom